W9-BAJ-708

Marie, Dancing

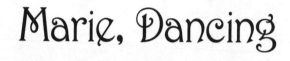

Marie, Dancing

Carolyn Meyer

Gulliver Books

Harcourt, Inc.

Orlando   Austin   New York   San Diego   Toronto   London

www.HarcourtBooks.com

Gulliver Books is a trademark of Harcourt, Inc., registered
in the United States of America and/or other jurisdictions.

Library of Congress Cataloging-in-Publication Data
Meyer, Carolyn, 1935–
Marie, dancing/Carolyn Meyer.
p. cm.
"Gulliver Books."
Summary: A fictionalized autobiography of Marie van Goethem,
the impoverished student from the Paris Opéra ballet school who became the
model for Edgar Degas's famous sculpture, "The Little Dancer."
[1. Ballet dancing—Fiction. 2. Degas, Edgar, 1834–1917—Fiction.
3. Poverty—Fiction. 4. Paris (France)—History—1870–1940—Fiction.
5. France—History—Third Republic, 1870–1940—Fiction.] I. Title.
PZ7.M5685Ma 2005
[Fic]—dc22 2004026547
ISBN-13: 978-0152-05116-7 ISBN-10: 0-15-205116-3

Text set in Fournier
Designed by Lydia D'moch

First edition
A C E G H F D B
Printed in the United States of America

Marie, Dancing is a work of fiction based on historical figures and events.
Some details have been altered to enhance the story.

For Michael and Lynn

Marie, Dancing

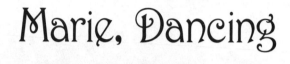

Paris, 1878

1

Monsieur Degas

ou," said the man wearing blue-tinted eyeglasses. "You, with the long braid. Come here, *s'il vous plaît*." He crooked a finger, beckoning. "If you please."

It was not an invitation; it was a command. I glanced around at the other dancers. "*Moi*, Monsieur?" I replied. "You mean *me*?"

"*Oui, oui—toi!*" the man growled impatiently. "Yes, I mean *you*, Mademoiselle."

I knew who he was, although he had never before spoken to me: Monsieur Degas, the artist. All the dancers of the Paris Opéra ballet knew Monsieur Degas. He was often at the Palais Garnier, present at our morning classes and our afternoon rehearsals, sitting on a wooden chair in the corner with a drawing pad open on his knees, watching us through those eyeglasses or a pince-nez perched on his long nose. His pencil skimmed over the paper, scarcely pausing. We thought him peculiar, an eccentric kind of person, and we generally ignored him. Had he been sketching me just now, as I scratched my back and yawned?

The afternoon rehearsal was finished; the dancers were changing out of their practice tutus and slippers and into street clothes and sabots. I was tired and hungry, eager to be gone. What did he want of me?

He didn't wait for me to reply or to change my clothes but simply walked off, motioning for me to follow. I snatched up my old tartan shawl and ran after him, my wooden clogs echoing through the poorly lit maze of corridors in the opera house.

It was my mother's desire that my sisters and I become dancers. I had passed my fourteenth birthday in February, and since the age of nine I had been enrolled as a student at the ballet school of the Paris Opéra. Antoinette—seventeen—and I were now members of the *corps de ballet;* Charlotte, just eight, was only a *petit rat,* a "little rat." Maman's dream of a better life for us had meant long hours and many sacrifices, a daily struggle to survive.

As we hurried along without speaking, Monsieur Degas a few steps ahead, I wondered if he would ask me to pose for him. He left the Palais Garnier and strode rapidly up Rue de la Chaussée d'Antin toward Place Pigalle. The street was steep and narrow. A cold mist hung in the air. Still dressed in my practice tutu, my sleeveless bodice, and tights with holes in the knees, I shivered and wrapped the ragged shawl, which had provided feasts for generations of moths, tighter around my shoulders.

That morning I had been practicing at the *barre*, the wooden railing that ran the length of the classroom wall— polished by hundreds of hands that had clutched it during exercises. I was performing an *arabesque*, balanced on my left leg, right leg extended out straight behind me, head up, right arm curving gracefully, fingers held just so. From this position I moved to an *attitude*, similar to an *arabesque* but with the right knee slightly bent. I was certain that every muscle in my body had memorized the small differences between the two. But at that moment Madame Théodore clapped her hands and shouted across the room in her terrible grating voice, "Marie! Mademoiselle van Goethem! What is it you're doing, Mademoiselle? You look like a dog pissing!"

I heard the other girls smother their laughter in muffled gasps. I disliked them for laughing, but if I had been in their place, no doubt I, too, would have laughed. A dozen times a day she shouted at me, as she did at them, but this was the worst. Madame Théodore taught by humiliation. You prayed that she would never look your way, but sooner or later she always did, and her eyes, sharp as needles, missed nothing. *Un chien pissant!*

Tears stung my eyes. I bowed my head while she lectured me, blood rushing to my face. I had vowed that I would never weep in front of her, as many of the girls had. When she was through with me, I resumed my position at the *barre*, and Madame Théodore turned her piercing eye and biting tongue on someone else.

Now I trotted behind Monsieur Degas—my sabots clattering on the damp cobblestones—wondering if we were going to his studio but afraid to ask, lest he think me impudent. Cane tucked under his arm and cloak flapping about his stooped shoulders, he marched up the narrow street like a general at the head of an army. He wasn't a young man, for his closely cropped beard was streaked with gray. Although he was such a familiar figure at our classes and rehearsals, none of the students of the ballet school had seen the pictures he'd made of us. My sister Antoinette had sometimes posed for him, and she'd heard that his paintings fetched high prices from wealthy collectors. Maybe *les étoiles*, the stars of the ballet, saw his pictures. But not us, the lowly dancers of no importance.

He didn't say a word to me until we turned onto Rue Frochot and stopped in front of number four, a tall, narrow door with chipped green paint. I knew the place: I had been there before. My mother worked as a laundress, and Monsieur Degas was one of her customers. Each week Maman sent me or my older sister to pick up a wicker basket full of dirty linens and, later, to return the clean linens, ironed and carefully packed in the same basket. I had never been farther than the first-floor landing, never encountered Monsieur

Degas himself; instead, I had handed the basket over to the housekeeper, Madame Sabine, and waited while she counted out the shirts and other linens, and then the *sous* that were owed. My sister Antoinette boasted that she had often been invited upstairs to his studio on the fifth floor.

"To model for him," she said. Then she added, "in the nude," and pursed her lips in an arch manner that made me want to pinch her.

I didn't know whether to believe her or not. Antoinette was a born liar. She'd lie for no particular reason, sometimes just to make herself look better or to make someone else look worse. I often lied, too, when I had something I wanted to hide, but I had to work at it and was never as successful as my sister. I didn't think it would have bothered Antoinette to take off her clothes for an artist. She was like that. I was certain it would bother me.

Now I followed Monsieur Degas up flight after flight of stairs. The higher we climbed, the more I worried what he might ask me to do and what I would say to him. When we reached the topmost floor, he pushed open the door on its creaking hinges. I hesitated. Only then did he turn to look at me. "My place of work," he said in his gravelly voice. "Come in."

I stepped over the high threshold and entered into chaos.

There were haphazard piles everywhere: dusty tutus; heaps of worn-out ballet slippers; a jumble of bowls, pitchers, books, and candlesticks; ladders; zinc bathing tubs; old wooden chairs; a small piano; a couple of violins and other musical instruments; a divan covered in dark red velvet rubbed bare of its nap. A battered worktable was strewn with tubes of paint, boxes of crayons, sticks of charcoal, jars of brushes, tangles of wire, and lumps of clay. A printing press with a large wheel occupied one corner. Several easels stood about like sentinels, some holding pictures; more pictures were stacked on the floor, facing the wall. I ran my fingertips along the edge of the worktable, and they came away gray with dust.

I don't believe Antoinette was here, I thought, gazing around the studio, *or she would have stolen something and flaunted it.*

Still wearing his hat and cloak, Monsieur Degas lit a gas lamp and seated himself on a tall wooden stool. He folded his arms across his chest and peered at me intently through his blue-tinted eyeglasses.

His steady gaze heightened my uneasiness. I wanted to turn and run down the stairs, but I lowered my eyes and forced myself to stay where I was. "Turn around," he said, and I hurried to do as he asked. "Slowly!"

I turned slowly.

A sound of disgust rattled in his throat. "Get rid of that shawl," he ordered, "and put on those slippers." He pointed to the heap of old ballet slippers. I put on the first pair I picked up. The shoes were too small, and cramped my toes, but I was too nervous to search for a better pair. I bent to tie the ribbons around my ankles.

"Hold that!" cried Monsieur Degas, already beginning to sketch.

He had caught me in an awkward position. "But, Monsieur . . . ," I protested.

"Do not move, Mademoiselle, *s'il vous plaît!*"

I tried to remain still, but I was tense and off-balance. He made that sound again—impatience, perhaps, rather than disgust. "Go over there." He pointed to a small wooden platform. "The model's stand. That's where I'll want you from now on."

I obeyed. He adjusted his stool and tossed aside his hat. "Fourth position!" He began to unbutton his cloak.

I settled into the familiar ballet position, one foot in front of the other, toes turned out.

"Lean back. Hands behind you. Clasp them. Good. Stretch your arms. Arch your back. More. That's better. Head up. Up!" He climbed down from the stool and took two long paces toward me. The quick movement startled me, and I stepped back, away from him. His eyes were large behind the blue lenses. He smelled of coffee and tobacco. "Don't move unless I tell you," he said quietly, reaching for my chin and tilting my face upward. "Now, again. Fourth position, Mademoiselle."

I tried to do exactly as he directed. He would step back and study me and then adjust my foot, my hands, my head. If I moved at all, he became irritated. The struggle to remain perfectly still was harder than I had expected.

"You'll do nicely," he said at last, and a hint of a smile passed over his lips, although his eyes seemed sad. "You will come here twice a week for three hours, oftener if I need you, less often if I do not. One franc each time. Agreed?"

"*Oui,* Monsieur Degas."

He opened a small gray notebook. "Your name and address?"

I told him, adding, "I'm the laundress's daughter. I've delivered your linens downstairs." I decided not to mention my sister Antoinette.

"Really?" he murmured in a disinterested way.

A bell rang, and from somewhere below a voice called, "Edgar? May I come up?"

Moments later a lady arrived, dressed in a handsome gray walking suit trimmed in black fur, breathless and smiling. Behind her, Madame Sabine, the housekeeper, labored up the stairs, puffing. A white muslin cap covered her gray hair and an apron was pinned to her large bosom. She carried a tray of pastries and a steaming pot of chocolate. The delicious smell reminded me that I'd had nothing to eat since the stale roll soaked in coffee that had been my breakfast.

Monsieur Degas greeted the lady with a kiss on both cheeks and began to clear a space on a table among a clutter of notebooks. Madame Sabine set down the tray. She saw me eyeing the pastries and shook her head, *non.* With a final warning look, she thumped back down the stairs.

The lady had taken off her elegant feathered bonnet and

set it on the velvet divan, next to her tightly furled silk umbrella. Now she unbuttoned her fine leather gloves and pulled them off, finger by finger. I couldn't help staring at her. She wasn't beautiful, but she was so stylish!

"See what I have here, Mary. What do you think, eh?" Monsieur Degas asked her. "A prize, *non?* Take a look at this girl's back!" He glanced at me. "Turn, *s'il vous plaît.*"

I did so.

"And look at that turnout! Superb, eh?" The two of them peered closely at my legs, toes pointed left and right, hip bones easy in their sockets.

Then he showed her the drawings he had made of me bending over to tie the slipper and standing on the model's stand.

"*Eh bien,* Edgar, a new painting, then?" the lady asked. She spoke French with a foreign accent. She had begun pouring the steaming chocolate into two china cups, so at ease that I believed she probably came here often. *They must be lovers,* I thought.

"Something new, indeed, but not a painting. A sculpture. Something entirely different. Something I've never tried before. It will have all of Paris talking. You'll see."

They began to discuss this new work he planned—a statuette, he called it, not life-sized but only about a meter high.

"You'll have it cast in bronze, then?" she asked.

"*Non, non,* I intend to leave it in wax, closer to human flesh."

"But that's not how you paint them, is it? As mere humans? The dancers in your pictures are more like sylphs or fairies. They're not bound by the laws of gravity, like ordinary mortals."

Monsieur Degas folded his arms across his chest. "When you sit in your box at the Palais Garnier, what you see on the stage is all beautiful illusion," he said. "For those hours on the stage, bathed in the glow of the footlights, the dancers are creatures of our imagination. But that's not the truth of it, Mary." He began to pace around the crowded room. "I haven't yet shown them as they really are: urchins, waifs forced to demand incredible things of their frail bodies. In this sculpture I want to show the truth, the grittiness of their lives."

He understands, I thought admiringly. *He knows that when we're dancing we leave this world behind for an hour or two or three, that we're free, and when we're dancing our best, it's the most wonderful feeling imaginable. But then it ends, and we crash to earth like injured birds.*

"But what about beauty, Edgar?" The lady gazed intently at Monsieur Degas. "Isn't that what the artist wishes to create?"

"Truth," Monsieur Degas repeated in his familiar growl. "Truth is what I'm after. Truth *is* beauty."

They had become so deeply engrossed in their conversation that Monsieur Degas and the lady seemed to have forgotten about me. I understood from the way she asked questions that she, too, was an artist. I stopped listening. In spite of Madame Sabine's warning look, I wondered if I might have a chance to snatch up one of the pastries so temptingly close. No one was paying the least bit of attention to me. I sidled nearer to the tray. My mouth watered and my fingertips tingled. My hand hovered near the pastries.

Suddenly the lady appeared beside me, smiling. Startled, I tucked both hands beneath my armpits. "I'm Mademoiselle Cassatt," she said. "And what's your name, *ma petite?*"

"Marie," I answered. "Marie van Goethem."

"And at what level do you dance, Marie?"

"The *premier quadrille*, Mademoiselle," I replied proudly, for I had attained this level within the *corps de ballet* at the autumn examinations. "My older sister dances with the *coryphées*," I said, referring to the more advanced group, "and my younger sister is just eight years old and in the *classe des petites*. My sisters are very talented," I added, because there was a kindness in the lady's face that encouraged me to tell her more than she had asked.

"I'm sure they are. And you, too, certainly!" She turned to Monsieur Degas. "Edgar, mightn't Marie have one of these lovely pastries? And my cup of chocolate as well. I'm really not in the least hungry, and the girl looks as though she could do with a bite."

I closed my eyes. The smell of chocolate made my stomach feel as though it were caving in on itself. But the thought of eating in front of this elegant lady, the artist's lover, was too much. "*Non, merci,* Mademoiselle," I mumbled and rushed to the door, nearly forgetting my shawl.

"Next week, then?" Monsieur Degas called after me as I ran down the stairs. I stopped and turned back to tell him *oui*. He loomed above me. "Tuesday we will begin. I will make you *une étoile,*" he announced. "A star."

Une étoile! How did he intend to accomplish that? But he was smiling, and I believed him—that somehow he would. "Until Tuesday!" I sang out.

THE LAUNDRY WHERE my mother worked was in a row of small shops in the passage behind our rooms on Rue de Douai. This was only a few streets away from Monsieur Degas's studio, but it might have been in a different world. Our street stank of rotting garbage and manure.

"You're late," Maman grumbled. "And why are you still in your practice clothes? Where were you? I had work for you."

"With Monsieur Degas," I said. "Is there anything to eat here?" I lifted the lid of a pot simmering on the back of the stove where the laundresses heated their irons. Chunks of cabbage, a few carrots, slices of onion, and several potatoes swam in a greasy broth. I reached for a bowl and spoon.

"Ah, Monsieur Degas! In his atelier? Does he want you to model?"

"*Oui,* Maman. For a sculpture, he says. A little statue." I didn't mention his promise to make me *une étoile,* because she might have laughed.

"How much?"

"One franc each time I pose."

"Nude or clothed?"

"He didn't say. Clothed, I think."

"You didn't ask?"

"*Non.* But I'll find out when I go back."

"He must pay you more if you're nude," Maman said.

"I don't want to pose nude," I said, turning away. The soup tasted terrible. I searched for a piece of bread.

"Don't be stubborn, Marie. He'll pay you more with your clothes off. How can you refuse when you know how much we need the money?" She set one flatiron back on the stove and picked up another, spit on her finger and tested it against the hot metal. The spit sizzled. Quickly she pressed a cuff, a sleeve, a second cuff. I knew she was waiting for an answer.

"It's all right for Antoinette," I said, fishing a carrot from the watery soup. There was no sign of meat. "Not for me."

"You think you're better than your sister, is that it?" Maman demanded, switching irons again. "But you're not."

I did think I was, but I bit my tongue and said nothing.

2

Foyer de la Danse

A few days after my first visit to Monsieur Degas's studio, Antoinette persuaded me to go with her to the *foyer de la danse,* between the acts of *Giselle.* Because I was only a member of the *quadrille,* the lowest level, I wasn't allowed in the ornate hall behind the great Opéra stage, where *coryphées* and *sujets*—dancers of the higher levels—gathered to warm up for performances and to relax during the interval between acts. But after hearing so much about it, I was curious and agreed to go.

Everyone knew the real purpose of the *foyer de la danse:* It was a meeting place for dancers and their admirers. Admission was a privilege offered only to *abonnés,* wealthy gentlemen who bought subscriptions for seats in the stalls behind the orchestra. (I'd heard that subscribers paid far more for a year's subscription than most dancers earned.) Ordinary male patrons were not admitted to the *foyer*, no female patrons were allowed, and dancers below the level of *coryphée* knew better than to try to get past the guards posted at the doors. Antoinette flouted this rule.

"Just follow me," Antoinette whispered. "Gilles, the guard with the drooping mustaches, won't say anything if you're with me. But once we're inside, you're on your own. No doubt my friend, Monsieur Chevreul, will want to chat with me. Just don't call attention to yourself, and no one will be the wiser."

While Antoinette distracted Gilles with her disarming smile, I slipped past him. Some of the *coryphées* recognized me but chose to ignore me. Even before the stars had finished making their *révérences* to the audience, gentlemen in black tailcoats and starched white shirtfronts—their gleaming black opera hats cradled in the crooks of their arms—began to swarm into the *foyer*. Soon every dancer had at least one or two admirers paying her compliments on her performance, the gentlemen hovering like black-and-white bees around brightly colored flowers.

For a little while I stood along the side, dazzled by the rich glow of gilded carvings and the glitter of the sparkling chandeliers multiplied over and over in the ornately scrolled mirrors along the walls. Then I discovered that by turning my back to the hall, I could watch the scene as it was reflected in the mirrors, without being observed myself. It was as though a second kind of dance had begun: The dancers flirted and smiled and the gentlemen in black laughed a little too loudly, showing their teeth.

Antoinette was right—no one paid me the least attention. With my back to the swirling crowd, it was as though I'd made myself invisible. Who would try to start a conversation with a girl who seemed entirely disinterested?

From this vantage point I could easily observe my sister and the gentleman with a gardenia in his buttonhole who leaned toward her so attentively. I assumed this was the Monsieur Chevreul she'd been talking about recently. *"Mon grand ami,"* she called him, "my great friend." I noticed the tilt of her chin, her lowered lashes, her charming pouts and smiles, all of which I had watched her practice at home in the speckled mirror that hung above the cracked washbasin. With her delicate features, eyes as cool and green as a cat's, and blond hair that flowed over her bare shoulders like satin, Antoinette was a beautiful flower, and Monsieur Chevreul— if that's who the man was—buzzed closer and closer.

After about an hour a porter appeared at the entrance of the *foyer,* ringing a bell to signal the end of the interval. I heard Antoinette's trilling laugh—she practiced that, too— as her "great friend" bowed low and pressed her hand to his lips. From my position I could see that he was nearly bald on top. *He would look better with a hat,* I thought.

Once the gentlemen had left to return to their seats and the dancers had done some warm-up exercises, the callboy, a wizened old fellow with a wispy white beard, stood at the door and proclaimed in his ancient singsong, "All on the stage for the second act! Curtain going up!" We hurried to take our places. As she flitted past me, Antoinette whispered, "Chevreul has invited me to join him tonight for supper after the performance."

The stage manager sent out an apprentice with a watering can to sprinkle the wooden floor so our feet wouldn't slip. The gasman turned down the cocks of the gas jets, dimming the lights in the *grande salle de spectacle*, and the orchestra struck up the first notes of the overture to act 2, drowning out the laughter and chatter of the audience. The *étoile* dancing the role of the peasant girl, Giselle—killed at the end of the first act by her own hand with Prince Albrecht's sword—climbed into her coffin. The stagehands hauled on the ropes to raise the great red velvet curtain, revealing the forest at night. A *premier sujet* made her entrance in the role of Myrtha, queen of the Wilis—virgins who had died unfulfilled and who now haunted the woods at night. Myrtha glided across the stage in a series of rapid *bourrée* steps, ending in an *arabesque*. In another few measures Giselle would arise, transformed into one of the Wilis. The Wilis—the rest of us in the *corps de ballet*—were dressed in long white tutus, symbolizing our purity. I made a final adjustment to the silk cord of my slipper and took several slow breaths to rid myself of the slight nervousness I always felt while waiting for my cue.

"You're to become ethereal creatures," our ballet master,

Monsieur Perrot, had reminded us at rehearsal. "You must float across the stage as though you were a cloud, your slippers barely touching the floor. It must appear effortless."

There was our cue: Queen Myrtha summoning the Wilis. *Float,* I told myself as I rose on *pointe* and lifted my arms above my head in third position. *Float,* I thought, and began the *bourrées,* sweeping onto the stage—no longer Marie van Goethem but a Wili, once again a part of the dance.

BACK IN THE DIRTY, crowded dressing room after the final curtain had been rung down, I pulled off my tutu, bodice, and tights, and wearing only my corset and drawers, handed the costume over to the wardrobe mistress, and my slippers to her assistant. "Worn how many times?" the assistant asked, examining the white slippers.

"Six," I lied. We were required to wear our pink slippers for ten performances, white for six, and then we could use the castoffs for class and rehearsals. My current practice slippers were completely broken down in the toe and made dancing on *pointe* very painful. I needed these newer shoes, but the assistant in charge cast me a weary look and shook her head, hanging the slippers on the rack to be worn again.

"Stitch the old ones," she said.

"I have," I replied. "I've stitched the toes several times." But I was wasting my breath. The old slippers would have to do.

————

ANTOINETTE had already left the Palais Garnier on the arm of Monsieur Chevreul. I walked slowly across Place de l'Opéra, which was crowded with horse-drawn carriages. The night was cool and clear, and the cafés were thronged with elegantly dressed gentlemen in evening clothes, and tightly corseted ladies in furs and sparkling jewels, skillfully maneuvering their wide flounced skirts and petticoats. I searched the crowd for my sister and her new admirer and thought I glimpsed Antoinette in her green silk dress sitting at a table at the fashionable Café de la Paix. I paused and stared until I realized the wearer of the green dress was not my sister after all. I did catch sight of Monsieur Degas at a table near the glass doors that opened to the street. Seated next to him was a gentleman I'd seen earlier in the *foyer de la danse*. Neither of them noticed me.

I moved on, turning north along one of the steep, narrow streets that led toward Rue de Douai. I had walked a number of blocks when I heard behind me the ring of hoofbeats and the rattle of carriage wheels on cobblestone. When I stepped aside to allow the carriage to pass, I saw that Monsieur Chevreul was driving, my sister beside him with her head resting lightly on his shoulder. I was sure she saw me, but she pretended not to, her attention solely on the gentleman. Where were they going? Maybe he was taking her to a café on Place Pigalle. I knew she would not be home for hours.

3

Becoming a Dancer

It was long past midnight when I reached Rue de Douai and climbed the dimly lit and rank-smelling stairs to our two squalid rooms. I tumbled onto the straw-filled mattress and curled up beside my younger sister, Charlotte. The extra space would vanish when Antoinette eventually crawled into the creaking wooden bed shared by the three of us, with me squeezed in the middle.

Tired as I was, sleep would not come. I rolled over and tried to make out Charlotte's features in the sliver of moonlight that filtered through the cracked and grimy windowpane. At the age of eight she still sometimes sucked her thumb like a baby. I touched her cheek and gently pulled the thumb from her mouth.

Antoinette was nine and I was nearly six when Charlotte

was born, a year after my parents left their village in Belgium for Paris, in search of a better life. Our father earned his living as a tailor, our mother then, as now, as a laundress. We were poor, but there was always plenty of food on the table and decent clothes on our backs.

My mother was ambitious, and she believed the best way to ensure her daughters' success in life was to send us to the ballet school of the Paris Opéra to become dancers. As soon as we were settled in our new home, Maman enrolled Antoinette. I was to be enrolled later, once Antoinette had been promoted to the *corps de ballet*. When Charlotte was old enough, she, too, would begin.

Meanwhile, I spent my days with my father, who doted on me and took me everywhere with him—even to the homes of tradesmen and civil servants and others of modest means, for whom he made low-priced suits. My mother had ambitions for my father, too, and often urged him to seek out a wealthier clientele who would be willing to pay high prices for fine tailoring.

"You waste your time on shoemakers and greengrocers who order a new suit for their wedding and their children's christenings and who wear that same suit to their grave," she would tell him, in a tone that was sometimes pleading, sometimes nagging. But Papa was content with his life and pretended to ignore my mother's complaints.

Then, a year after I had begun my studies as a *petit rat*, my father fell ill and was no longer able to work. During his illness I rushed home from classes at the Opéra to spend every moment I could with him. He told me stories I had never heard about our family, particularly about my mother, who was the daughter of a prosperous lace maker in Brussels. She had fallen in love with my father when he was only a tailor's apprentice and eloped with him. Their life together had been a struggle from the start.

"Your mother was a beautiful young woman, brimming with vitality and good humor," he told me. "But she wasn't accustomed to hard work. She found her new circumstances very difficult."

I nodded, thinking of Maman and how worn-out she always appeared. It was hard to imagine her young and beautiful and carefree. *Like Antoinette,* I thought.

The week before he died, my father called me to his bedside. "Marie," he whispered, clutching my hand with what little strength he had left, "much will now rest on your young shoulders. Your mother is a good woman, but she is weak. Antoinette is beautiful, but I'm sad to say, she is becoming very selfish." He paused, and I wet his dry lips with a few drops of water.

"Shhhh," I whispered. "There's no need to speak, dear Papa. Save your strength."

But he seemed determined to say what was on his mind. "Charlotte is little more than a baby. You may still be young and small, but I know that you have a great heart. I've asked your godmother, my sister Hélène, to help you any way she can, but your mother has never been fond of her." I nodded again; Maman always felt that Tante Hélène looked down on her.

Papa had grown weaker, his breath coming in ragged gasps. I leaned closer to catch his words. "You—my good, sweet, dearest Marie—I'm asking you to hold the family together. Will you promise me that?"

I looked into my beloved papa's pain-filled eyes and promised. "*Oui, mon cher* Papa," I said, squeezing his hand. "I will do all that I can."

His mouth formed the words: *I know you will.*

AFTER MY FATHER'S DEATH, our life became much harder. My parents' small savings were gone. Often there wasn't enough to eat. But the worse it got for us, the more determined our mother was that all three of her daughters become dancers with the Opéra.

Tante Hélène tried to help us, as my father wished, but she disapproved of Maman's plan for us. I overheard the arguments when Tante Hélène came to visit us from *la rive gauche,* the Left Bank of the river Seine, where she had a workroom for dressmaking and plain sewing.

"Don't be a fool, Louise," Tante Hélène told my mother. "You're condemning your daughters to a life in the gutter. Surely you know that most of those little dancers end up selling their bodies and losing their souls."

"Mind your own business," Maman snapped. "My girls

will succeed. You think it's better for them to spend their lives bent over a laundry tub and a hot iron?"

"They could become seamstresses. I'd be happy to employ them and teach them all they need to know. It would at least be an honest trade until they marry."

My mother didn't bother to argue. She simply turned away.

"Don't say I didn't warn you, Louise," said my aunt.

"Hélène tries to interfere," Maman complained to us after our aunt had stormed out. "She thinks she's better than us. I can't bear her."

Although I liked this aunt and the gifts she often brought us—a comb, a length of ribbon, and best of all, a sack of sugared almonds—as I got older, I mostly agreed with Maman. I didn't want to be a seamstress, fingers sore from needle pricks, eyes bleary from long days spent squinting over a hem or a seam. And I wanted to be a laundress even less.

I loved to dance, even though there were times when I wondered if the exquisite joy of dancing was worth the endless drudgery of classes and rehearsals and the pain of sore muscles and aching feet. I had learned that a dancer's life was harsh, exhausting, and often painful, and paid little unless you were an *étoile* or at least a *premier sujet*. We resented our teacher, Madame Théodore, for criticizing us so severely, and Monsieur Perrot, the ballet master, for driving us without mercy, but we depended on them completely.

When Charlotte was old enough to begin her studies at the Opéra, she never seemed to question her future. "I will do whatever I must to become a dancer," she told me gravely, her innocent gray eyes earnest, her sweet mouth set in a stubborn line. And now, on nights when the audience filled the *grande salle de spectacle* and I leaped and skimmed across the stage, I knew that she was right. Dancing was truly the only thing that mattered.

I DOZED A LITTLE but woke up with a start when Antoinette stumbled into our room, cursing as she bumped into, first, a chair and then the dresser. I listened to the rustle of silk as she yanked off her dress and tossed it aside, then to the hiss as she used the chamber pot.

"Are you awake, Marie?" she whispered as she sank heavily onto the mattress beside me. I smelled wine on her breath.

I didn't answer, pretending to be asleep, but she wasn't fooled.

"You saw him, didn't you? My gentleman friend? Not bad, eh? I'm sure he likes me. And he's a rich one!" She pinched me through my flimsy chemise. "Answer me, Marie. You're awake, I know."

"Mmmmm," I said.

"Chevreul is a banker, and very, very generous," she purred contentedly. She spread a handful of francs over her thin pillow. "He gave me this. As a gift of friendship," she added. "I'm to buy a new dress." She swept the money into a little leather purse, which she tucked under the mattress.

"Good," I said. "Now let me sleep."

4

Rehearsal on the Stage

Maman shook us on her way out the next morning, calling that we must not be late for class. Only Charlotte awoke with a smile, her cherubic face rumpled with sleep. I felt exhausted, as I often did on the day after a performance. Our schedule called for us to dance three times each week: Monday, Wednesday, and Saturday nights. Performances began at nine o'clock and ended long after midnight. Regardless of when we got home, we had to be at class by nine the next morning and were fined if we were even a few minutes late. I nearly always managed to arrive before Madame Théodore began her instruction, but Antoinette sometimes gave up a big part of her salary to fines.

When Antoinette merely sighed and burrowed deeper beneath the scanty blanket, Maman threatened to beat her, shouting that she was a selfish, worthless daughter. I added my voice, begging Antoinette to think for once of the rest of us. The door slammed behind Maman. Charlotte's eyes welled with tears.

Antoinette shrugged it off. "It's nothing to me," she muttered. "I can make up for it in other, more interesting ways."

I finished plaiting my hair in a single braid and tied it with a length of frayed ribbon. *Chevreul,* I thought as Charlotte and Antoinette argued. *He'll pay her fine.*

"Mon Dieu!" I said in a low voice. "Your fighting doesn't fill our stomachs!" But Antoinette pulled the pillow over her head.

I opened the cupboard and found half a loaf of stale bread to soak in the coffee Maman had left in a tin pot on the gas ring. The milk on the windowsill had begun to sour. *Is this all?* I wondered. It was hardly enough to sustain us. I knew Maman had been drinking again. Angrily I banged the pot back onto the fire. Her drinking had once more robbed us of what little money we earned.

Luckily, there was still a spoonful of sugar in a jar. I divided the stale bread among three cracked and chipped bowls, sprinkled the slices with sugar, poured coffee over them, and added the milk. I gave Charlotte her portion, adding half of mine to it as well, and left the rest for

Antoinette, for whenever she finally got her bones out of bed.

I poked Antoinette as Charlotte and I were leaving for the Palais Garnier. "Another fine for you, my girl," I said, but there was no reply. Charlotte and I raced down the dirty stairs, slamming the door behind us.

FOR ONCE Madame Théodore had nothing cruel to say to me, her glittering eye fixed on someone else in the *premier quadrille*. We finished an hour of exercises at the *barre*, beginning with *pliés* and *demi-pliés*, knee bends to improve the turnout of the legs from the hips, in the five ballet positions. Next we practiced the *développé*—the slow unfolding of the legs, every movement smooth and controlled—followed by the *attitude* (*un chien pissant!*) and the *arabesque*. I scarcely had a chance to wonder when Antoinette had arrived at the *coryphées'* class down the hall, and how much she'd been fined this time.

We proceeded to the center floor, repeating the same exercises without the *barre* to aid our balance, and worked on *port de bras*—positions of the arms—and combinations of movements, both slow and fast. Toward the end of the class, the tempo increased to allegro. We traveled diagonally across the floor by twos, practicing dainty little *bourrées* on *pointe*, and turns—*pirouettes* and *fouettés;* then jumps—*grands jetés, pas de chat, entrechats*. This was my favorite part: I loved to jump!

Monsieur Degas sat in his usual corner, dressed in a pepper-and-salt suit and a floppy black tie. If he recognized me, he gave no sign. I pretended to ignore him, although in fact I was watching him closely.

He didn't try to draw us while we were perfecting a *pirouette* or a *fouetté* turn. He didn't try to freeze the moment when we were soaring in a *grand jeté*, light as birds in the air. Instead, he waited until we had collapsed on benches or sprawled on the floor, mere wingless humans. When we were half dead with fatigue, our legs too tired to carry us through one more jump, our arms aching, our feet sore from balancing on *pointe* in worn-out shoes—that was when he began to draw.

I didn't understand. Why did he want to show us at our worst? Where was the art in that? "Truth is what I am after," he had said to Mademoiselle Cassatt. And this made me wonder: In the statuette he planned to make of me, would I look awkward, even ugly? I wasn't beautiful like Antoinette. I didn't have Charlotte's sweet innocence. Monsieur Degas promised to make me *une étoile*, a star, and I hoped he'd somehow keep his word. I wanted to look graceful and elegant, like someone who might be admired by his lover, Mademoiselle Cassatt.

Naturally I said nothing as we three sisters walked home from the Opéra that Thursday afternoon. I could imagine how Antoinette would scoff if I ever confessed that I wanted to impress the lady artist.

"What good can such a lady do you?" she would ask scornfully. "Will she give you money? Buy you jewelry and clothes? Take you out to dine? Are you crazy, Marie? You must find yourself a gentleman, someone like Monsieur Chevreul, and the sooner the better."

FINALLY IT WAS Saturday, with a performance that night and then a whole day of rest. When there was no performance, the dancers of each level rehearsed separately, but on performance days the entire *corps de ballet* gathered on the stage of the Palais Garnier for the afternoon rehearsal. I loved being there at night, when the enormous chandelier that hung suspended from the painted ceiling was lit, dozens of little gaslights pouring their brilliant yellow glow onto the crowd below. On three sides of the *grande salle,* tiers of gilded boxes rose like balconies; the boxes were occupied by ladies in silks and jewels, who leaned forward to inspect the audience through opera glasses, knowing that they in turn were being inspected. But during rehearsals the gilded boxes remained empty, the orchestra pit on the other side of the footlights was deserted, and the *grande salle* yawned dark and silent.

A full orchestra would play that night, but now we had only Monsieur Dufresne, the violinist, and Monsieur Perrot, the ballet master, pounding out the tempo with his wooden staff. No matter how many times I had been on that stage—Perrot claimed it was the largest, not only in France but in all of Europe—I was always awed by the vastness of it, by the painted flats of scenery that rose up from slots in the floor or dropped down from the high ceiling or slid in from the *coulisses,* the wings. The floor itself was slanted to give the audience a better view of our legs and feet, and we had to adjust to the slant after dancing on the level floor of the practice room.

We were dancing certain parts of Meyerbeer's opera, *Robert le diable.* The star, a beautiful Italian ballerina, was beyond our jealousy, but the *premiers sujets* who danced the minor solo roles stirred the envy of us all, not only because of the choice parts they were assigned and the admiration they received, but because of the money they were paid—6,800 francs or more a year! At the level below, the *petits sujets* danced in small groups, and the *coryphées,* ranked below them, were in turn desperately envied by those of us in the *quadrille.* We were all determined to move up to join them as soon as possible. While we were assembled on the great stage, though, our jealousy and ambition had to be set aside for the sake of the dance. The dance was everything.

After rehearsal, in one of the practice rooms where the dancers rested before putting on the costumes and makeup for the evening performance, Antoinette invited me to share her supper—a savory meat pie, a nice piece of cheese, a fresh roll—cutting each item in two with a little ivory-handled knife. "Courtesy of Monsieur Chevreul," she said with a wink. "And look—there's even an apple tart."

I sensed that she wanted me to ask about her "great friend," but I stubbornly refused. "The meat pie is delicious," I said—that was all the satisfaction I would grant her.

"*Oui, c'est vrai,*" said Antoinette, her mouth full. "True enough. But you should have seen the dinner we had the other night. Asparagus soup, *rissoles* of rabbit with truffles, saddle of venison, galantine of guinea fowl in jelly, pineapple fritters . . ."

"How can you tell me such a story, when the rest of us are so hungry?" I cried.

Antoinette merely shrugged. "Come with me tonight to the *foyer de la danse*. Chevreul will be there to meet me. If you wouldn't behave so strangely, maybe you'd meet someone, too."

"*Non, merci.*"

"And why not?"

"Because I'm tired," I said. "And besides, I'm not interested."

"Don't be stupid, Marie," Antoinette scolded. "You're wasting opportunities. You're not a natural flirt, that's the trouble. You need to practice the art of seduction, so that in another two or three years, when you're a little older, you'll be ready to find yourself a fine gentleman. As it is now, you exhibit about as much charm as an old broom. And charm is what it's all about, you know. You're never going to get anywhere at this rate."

"I'll get wherever I'm going without your advice," I said sharply. "And I have no intention of visiting the *foyer* ever again." I couldn't resist asking, "By the way, how much were you fined today for being late?"

Antoinette ignored the question. Instead she smiled knowingly. "What a stubborn, headstrong child you are! But you'll learn, Marie. Someday you'll look back and say, 'Antoinette, you were right.' Because you know that I am." She hesitated and then added, "Fifty centimes—not much."

I wanted so much to slap her—any amount was too much! Instead, I got up and walked away, leaving her with the entire apple tart.

5

Le Rat Mort

As I dawdled slowly toward home an hour past midnight, several of my friends from the *premier quadrille*—Geneviève and Léonie and Mathilde—caught up with me. They were in a merry mood, laughing and talking, happy that the next day, Sunday, was our day off.

"Come, Marie," said Léonie, linking her arm with mine. "We're off to le Rat Mort to treat ourselves to something to eat and drink. You must join us."

I was tempted, but I had not yet begun to pose for Monsieur Degas and hadn't a single *sou* in my pocket.

"Don't worry," said Geneviève, whose mother was a milliner and who had more money than most of us, "I'll pay for yours as well."

I hesitated for only a moment before I agreed, promising that in the future I would do the same for her.

Le Rat Mort—the Dead Rat—a café open all hours of the day and night, was frequented by artists, writers, models, and dancers accompanied by gentlemen they'd met at the *foyer de la danse*. Women of bad reputation were known to stop at the Rat at the end of a long night on the streets. The food was cheap, and the proprietress and her husband sometimes let customers run up a bill that could be paid later.

We indulged ourselves, ordering bread and pâté and cheese, and coffee thick with cream. Never mind that the bread was a day old, the pâté and cheese dry at the edges, the coffee bitter—we were pleased to have it.

"Look!" Léonie whispered loudly. "There's Suzanne!"

We turned to stare at the tall, willowy girl in a little fur-trimmed bonnet who had entered on the arm of a short gentleman in evening dress, with bushy side-whiskers and a monocle in his left eye. Suzanne had begun ballet classes with us years earlier, yet she had somehow risen past us, promoted at the autumn examinations to the level of *petit sujet*.

"I will never understand how she got that promotion," Mathilde grumbled. "She's not really much of a dancer."

"It's because of her looks," Léonie said with conviction. "Her slender legs and the way she smiles and tosses her curls."

"Her *entrechats* are clumsy," Geneviève insisted. "Her *chaîné* turns are truly embarrassing."

"Have you watched her *fouettés?*" Mathilde asked, licking her spoon. The overweight orange tabby that resided at le Rat Mort stared up at us with luminous eyes and then leaped onto Mathilde's lap. "This old cat is more graceful than our Suzanne," Mathilde remarked, brushing the tabby onto the floor.

The spring examinations were coming up soon; they were traditionally held the week after Easter. We worked hard to prepare and prayed that we would pass, each of us believing that we were just as good as Suzanne—maybe even better. We sipped our coffee and criticized the dancers at every level above us. Then the conversation shifted to the *foyer de la danse* that, although we were forbidden to enter, was always a subject of gossip.

"We know you were there the other night," said Geneviève. "Tell us about it."

"There's nothing to tell," I said. My friends looked at each other and shrugged, smirking. "I went with Antoinette and stood in a corner while she flirted, and that was it. I'm never going back," I insisted.

My friends laughed. Their disbelieving laughter annoyed me, but I was determined to ignore it. "She left with Monsieur Chevreul, didn't she?" Léonie asked. Everyone knew about Antoinette and Monsieur Chevreul. Such things were never a secret. "My sister was his mistress for a short time," Léonie went on. "She used to complain about his nervous laugh. She said it gave her a headache. Has Antoinette mentioned that?"

I shook my head. I didn't want to discuss my sister and her gentleman, but I was curious. "He's kind, though, isn't he? He didn't mistreat her?"

"*Mais oui*. Very kind. Generous, too."

"Then why aren't they still together? Did she dump him because of his laugh?"

Léonie lifted her hands in a shrug. "She didn't dump *him;* he dumped *her*. Because his wife disapproved, I think."

His *wife?* I wondered if Antoinette knew about Madame Chevreul.

We ordered more coffee and more food. I felt less tired, and my spirits rose. Then I suddenly caught sight of my mother, sitting at a table across the room. I could see the glass of bright green liqueur in front of her: absinthe. It was obvious that this was not her first glass, or even her second or third. Cheaper than wine and deadly, absinthe was known as "the serpent with green eyes." All of the pleasure drained out of the evening. The change in my mood seemed to affect everyone. The high spirits at our table fell, and we became sullen. We no longer joked about Suzanne and made ourselves feel superior to her. The weariness returned, my legs felt heavy as logs, and I decided to go home.

I said good night and started for the door, but at the last moment I hesitated. How could I leave Maman there in such a state? Reluctantly I walked over to the table where my mother sat with two laundresses who worked with her.

Maman peered up at me from under drooping eyelids, her expression dull. Groggily she asked, "Marie? That you, *chérie*? You should be in bed, eh?"

"*Oui, c'est vrai*, Maman," I agreed. "Come. Let's go home."

"*Un moment.*" She drained her glass and pushed herself unsteadily to her feet. The two laundresses, also drunk, turned away and pretended not to watch. I took my mother's arm and steered her toward the door.

"*À bientôt*," my friends murmured, nodding sympathetically as we passed their table. "See you later." *We all have our troubles*, their eyes said.

We made our way slowly toward Rue de Douai, steering a crooked course and saying little. I helped my mother climb the stairs, and once I had eased her onto her couch and covered her with a ragged quilt, I dropped into bed, too weary even to bother undressing.

Half asleep, Charlotte reached for my hand. "I'm hungry, Marie," she whispered. "I couldn't find anything. My belly hurts."

"In the morning, *ma petite*," I told her, drawing her close into the curve of my arm. "Sleep now, and I'll get something for you then."

I felt ashamed that I had forgotten about my little sister and that I'd had a good supper with my friends while she went to bed with an empty stomach. Perhaps I could have gone back to the Rat and bought something for her, but I had no money, and by now my friends had surely gone. In minutes exhaustion overcame me, and even shame couldn't keep me awake.

ANTOINETTE CAME HOME sometime before dawn. She and Charlotte were both still asleep when I climbed over Antoinette and rinsed my face and hands in the washbasin. I checked the cupboard and found that Charlotte was right— there was nothing at all to eat. Creeping close to the bed, I slid my hand beneath the mattress, groping until I found Antoinette's little leather purse. In it were the francs given her by Monsieur Chevreul. I helped myself to a few of the smaller coins, replaced the purse, and started down the foul-smelling stairs. From habit, I held my breath until I reached the street.

It was early—the street sweepers were wielding their brooms on Rue Fontaine—but la Rochefoucauld market was already crowded. Women with untidy hair, still in slippers and dressing gowns, were bargaining over the price of stewing fowl and questioning the freshness of heaps of spring scallions.

I went from stall to stall with Antoinette's money, buying a packet of coffee and a jar of milk. The baker gave me a good price on a half dozen rolls left from the day before. After much deliberation, I bought four eggs—one for each of us. The egg vendor kindly added a small lump of butter wrapped in a bit of paper.

I hardly noticed the smudged and sickly tan paint of the stairway as I raced up to our rooms. I placed the beautiful brown eggs in a blue bowl on the table and gazed at them lovingly while I considered what to do next. I knew scarcely anything about cooking, because we had the habit of eating whatever was to be found in the cupboard. An omelet would be nice, but I had no idea how to make one. Should I boil the eggs instead? Then it came to me: I'd fry them in the butter.

While I was searching for a suitable pan, Maman lurched into the room. She looked terrible, her eyes red rimmed and puffy, her hair uncombed. She was moaning softly and clutching her head.

"Maman, what's wrong?" I asked, although I knew—it was the absinthe. "Are you ill?"

"I'd be better off dead!" she wailed. She lost her balance and stumbled against the table, knocking over the blue bowl. The eggs rolled out. I managed to catch two of them, but the others fell to the floor. The golden yolks splattered everywhere.

"Sorry," my mother muttered. "So sorry."

"You stupid woman!" I cried, exasperated beyond endurance. But I immediately felt ashamed—she was my mother, after all.

Maman got down on her knees, trying to scoop up the mess. I knelt beside her. "I didn't mean that," I said, although indeed it was how I felt. Couldn't she at least *try* to take care of her family?

Charlotte and Antoinette appeared in the doorway. "What?" Charlotte asked, staring at us with frightened eyes. "What happened?"

I shook my head, unable to find the words.

"You took my money," Antoinette said accusingly. "And now look what you've done!"

"Not Marie's fault," Maman muttered. "All mine." Sitting on the dirty floor, she began to weep, great wrenching sobs.

I touched her cheek. "It's all right, Maman," I murmured.

"No, it's *not* all right, Marie! She's always drunk!" Antoinette turned and stormed out of the room.

Charlotte's lip was trembling. "I'll get a rag," she said, "and help you clean it up."

6

The Studio on Rue Frochot

On the day I was to begin posing for Monsieur Degas, I threw my tartan shawl over my practice clothes and rushed from the Opéra to the studio at 4 Rue Frochot. The *quadrille* had had a special rehearsal that lasted longer than usual, and I was late. Madame Sabine answered the jingling bell.

"Go on up," she muttered.

When I reached the top floor, I knocked and waited, listened, and knocked again. After the third knock, I tried the door, found it unlatched, and pushed it open. "Monsieur Degas?" I called softly. I was answered by silence. "Monsieur Degas?" I repeated, louder this time, and then stepped inside.

Nothing seemed to have changed since I had been there a week earlier. The tray with the chocolate pot and pastries was still on the table, the chocolate dried on the delicate china cups, the remains of the half-eaten pastries stale and hard. I barely hesitated before cramming the stale bits into my mouth. I lifted the lid of the chocolate pot. A little dark liquid remained in the bottom, covered by a thin, wrinkled skin. I poured the thick, cold chocolate into one of the cups, drank it down, and wiped my mouth on the back of my hand.

I began to explore the studio. On one of the easels stood a painting of a dance class with several dancers practicing at the *barre*—I thought I recognized Antoinette—while other dancers held their positions in the center. Monsieur Degas had given the dancers in the painting black ribbons around their throats and colorful sashes around their waists; their gauzy tutus were crisp and bright, not like our shabby practice tutus. Two figures standing near a window and looking bored might have been Léonie and Geneviève. The only person I could identify positively was Monsieur Perrot, leaning on his wooden staff.

There were several pictures that seemed only partly finished. In one, a woman climbed out of a bathing tub—the actual zinc tub sat nearby in the studio. In another, men in black opera hats watched from the *coulisses* at the Opéra. I was excited to find pictures of laundresses bending over their flatirons or carrying baskets of linens, and I expected to see my mother or one of the other laundresses. But instead I recognized Emma, an older dancer retired from the Opéra, as the model.

Monsieur Degas's drawing pad lay open on his worktable. I lifted each page and examined it. There were sketches of slippered feet in various ballet positions, of hands poised like birds' wings, of heads tilted this way and that. There were detailed drawings of one dancer in *grand battement,* her right leg raised high; and of another dancer slumped on a bench with feet splayed, elbows propped on her knees, her weariness evident in a few pencil strokes.

Then I came to the drawings he had done of me during my first visit. The features were blurry, but there was my single, thick braid. In some sketches I looked awkward, even clumsy, but in others I thought I appeared very graceful. How strange it was, to see myself as Monsieur Degas must have seen me.

I was careful to replace the drawings exactly as I had found them, and I turned to a notebook lying nearby. I paged through it, although I could make out almost nothing, for I had not been taught to read or write. But I did recognize the most recent entry on an otherwise clean page: MARIE VAN GOETHEM RUE DE DOUAI 1 FR.

One franc—the amount I was to be paid each time I posed for him.

Curious, I flipped through earlier pages and found my sister's name: ANTOINETTE VAN GOETHEM RUE DE DOUAI 1 FR 40.

So she *had* been here! And he'd paid her one franc, forty centimes—more than he planned to pay me. *Why?* I thought

I knew—she posed without clothes. I slapped the notebook shut.

Suddenly I felt very tired. I shoved aside a pile of draperies on the velvet divan and sat down. Thinking I'd rest for a moment, I wrapped myself in my shawl, sank back against a cushion, and closed my eyes.

"Wake up!" a gravelly voice was saying loudly into my ear. "Mademoiselle Marie! Wake up!"

My eyes flew open. When I realized where I was, I felt embarrassed and also a little frightened. What if Monsieur Degas was angry that I had come into his studio without his permission? Suppose he now decided that I shouldn't model for the statuette after all! What if I had ruined everything?

I leaped to my feet, offering apologies, but Monsieur Degas brushed them aside. "If you are sufficiently rested, Mademoiselle," he said dryly, "shall we proceed with the session?"

I was dressed in a patched and mended skirt and a yellowed chemise that was once Antoinette's. "You wish me to wear a dance costume, Monsieur?" I asked. I began rummaging through the pile of dusty tutus.

The artist had hung up his frock coat and put on a long smock, such as those worn by housepainters. Clapping a battered felt hat onto his head, he said, "I wish you to wear nothing at all, Mademoiselle."

I stood rigidly silent, clutching one of the tutus. *Non*, I thought; *I can't do this.* My throat felt thick, and when I tried to swallow, I could not. Maman's words came back to me: *He must pay you more if you're nude.*

I thought again of Charlotte. She needed so many things! Forty centimes could make a difference.

Monsieur Degas was regarding me curiously. "*Eh bien*, Mademoiselle? What is it? We're wasting time."

I cleared my throat nervously. "It's a matter of money, Monsieur," I replied. "I must charge you an additional fifty centimes each time I remove my clothes." *Ten centimes more than Antoinette.*

"Certainly," he said. He opened the notebook and jotted something on the page with my name. "*Alors*, when you are ready, Mademoiselle."

There was a folding screen near the model's stand. Before I could change my mind, I stepped behind it and quickly re-moved the skirt, the chemise, the corset and drawers. I looked down at my naked body—thin but strong, my breasts small, my muscles smooth and taut from years of training. I worried what Monsieur Degas would think when he saw me. Maybe he would decide that I was too thin. Would he still want me to pose for him? I was shivering, partly from ner-vousness, partly because the studio was so cold, when I stepped out from behind the screen.

Monsieur Degas was shoveling charcoal into the small ce-ramic stove. I climbed onto the model's stand and faced him, attempting to shield my nakedness with my hands. I closed my eyes, drew a deep breath, opened my eyes again.

"I'm ready, Monsieur."

"*Bien,*" he said, his back still turned. "Good."

He took his time stoking the stove. When he had finished, he pulled up a tall wooden stool. He reached into a pocket for his pince-nez, which he perched on his nose. For a long time he eyed me critically, pulling on his lower lip as he studied my body from head to foot. I willed myself to be calm, but I could not stop trembling.

"Quarter turn, *s'il vous plaît,* Mademoiselle." I turned. "*Encore.*" I turned again, so that my back was now to the artist. "Once more."

As before, just as if I were fully clothed in tights and a tutu, Monsieur Degas had me assume some of the basic ballet positions. He barked out his commands: "*Arabesque,* Mademoiselle! *Écarté* front! *Développé!*" With each new command he instructed me to hold the position for what seemed like a very long time, to be as motionless as if I were a statuette. Sometimes he would approach me and peer closely at the standing leg or at my lifted arms. Then he would go back to his stool and his drawing pad.

Until he thought of something else, he always ordered me to return to the fourth position, the position in which a dancer is most at ease. In the fourth position I could be still. But I clenched my teeth when he touched me to change the placement of my arms or the angle of my head.

He studied and sketched, studied and sketched. The room grew warmer. Oddly, I found that his frank gaze did not embarrass me. My self-consciousness gradually disappeared. My nakedness was nothing more to him than a means for making a sculpture. He inspected me as carefully as my mother had inspected the goose she bought for our Christmas dinner long ago. My neck began to ache from the unaccustomed strain of holding the pose. To distract myself from the discomfort, I thought of that Christmas goose and the feast we'd had in a happier time, before my father had died, before my mother had begun to drink so heavily and had lost her way.

Downstairs a bell jangled, pulling me back to the present moment, and soon a familiar voice called up from below: "Edgar? It's Mary, and Lydia is with me. May we come up?"

"*Oui, oui,* come on up, Mesdemoiselles!" he shouted. To me he said, "Fourth position, *s'il vous plaît.*"

"*Non,* Monsieur, I . . . I can't," I stammered, rushing behind the screen.

I emerged fully clothed just as the door opened and Mademoiselle Cassatt entered the studio. She was dressed in a suit of cream-colored wool with a thin black stripe. The woman with her wore a velvet bonnet decorated with a curling black feather. Monsieur Degas greeted them with kisses on both cheeks and helped the second lady to a seat on the divan.

Mademoiselle Cassatt smiled at me as she removed her gloves. "Marie? Is that correct?"

"*Oui*, Mademoiselle," I said, pleased that she remembered my name.

"My sister, Mademoiselle Lydia Cassatt," she said, indicating the second lady, who was struggling to catch her breath and managed only a nod. I thought she looked unwell. I wondered if she, too, was an artist.

Mademoiselle Mary Cassatt began studying the sketches Monsieur Degas had made that afternoon as he spread them out on the table. Their attention was fixed entirely on those drawings. From time to time she would murmur, "Oh, look at that! Absolutely superb, Edgar." She didn't seem shocked by the nakedness of the girl in the drawings. "Lyddie, you must come take a look at these. They're simply exquisite."

The sister shook her head. "In a moment," she said. "When I'm myself again."

Curious to see them as well, I edged nearer. Mademoiselle Mary moved closer to Monsieur Degas to make room for me. "Of course you'd like to see them, too, wouldn't you, Marie? They're quite beautiful."

She was right—the pictures *were* beautiful.

"Which pose do you intend to use, Edgar?" she asked.

"Fourth position," he said. "Without question."

"Excellent. I'm sure it will be a great success." She smiled at him and touched his sleeve. I observed the way her fingers caressed the cloth of his old painter's smock, but he didn't respond to his lover's touch. He seemed not even to notice.

Mademoiselle Cassatt moved away and began talking about her work. She told Monsieur Degas about a painting she had begun of a little girl in a blue armchair. "I'm planning to submit it to the Universal Exposition next month."

"And is it going well?" he asked.

"I think it is, but I would be immensely grateful if you would come to my studio and take a look at it. The background is so . . ." She made a vague gesture with her hands. "Perhaps you could make some suggestions."

"*Oui,* of course I will."

Then Mademoiselle Lydia Cassatt joined their conversation, and Monsieur Degas described a picture he wanted to do of the two sisters on a visit to the Louvre, the great art museum by the Seine. "You'll pose here for the sketches. You'll be seated, Lydia, so there will be no strain. And you, Mary, will be seen only from the back."

"The back!"

"Very smart. Very refined. Trust me."

"*Bien entendu.* Of course, Edgar."

The first sister, Mary, was agreeable, but the frail Lydia seemed reluctant. They had forgotten about me entirely, but I didn't mind, because I was still gazing at the drawings he had done of me. I wished I could have one as a souvenir. I wondered if he ever threw away his drawings or tore them to pieces and fed them to the fire. Would he notice if I took one?

With a start I realized that Monsieur Degas was speaking to me. "Mademoiselle? Until next time, then?" He reached into his pocket and doled out the coins.

As I left the studio that evening with a franc and fifty centimes jingling in the pocket of my skirt, I wondered if I should tell Maman that I had posed nude. Maman would want to know if I'd been paid extra, and if I told her the truth, I'd have to hand over the extra fifty centimes. And so I decided not to tell her, but to deposit the additional coins in a secret tin I kept hidden at the tobacconist's shop in our building.

7

Dance Examinations

The spring dance examinations hung over our heads like an angry storm cloud.

Twice each year every student and member of the *corps de ballet*, from the youngest *rat* to the most seasoned soloist, had to submit to scrutiny by the Opéra jury. There were three possible outcomes for the dancer: to be promoted to the next level and given a higher wage, to stay where she was, or to be dropped from the *corps* entirely. Because I had advanced to the *premier quadrille* at the autumn examinations, I wasn't eligible for promotion; my hope was simply to pass. We had our fingers crossed, though, that Charlotte would be promoted from the *classe des petites* to the *classe des grandes* and made a regular member of the *corps de ballet*.

I lay awake for most of the night before the examinations,

while on either side of me my two sisters slept soundly. How could they? Toward morning I climbed out of our bed and crept into the other room. I found Maman at the table, hunched over a mug of coffee. "What are you doing up so early?" I asked.

"I might ask you the same question, *chérie*," said Maman. "Too nervous to sleep."

"*Moi, aussi,*" I sighed. "Me, too." I poured myself some tepid coffee and sat down across from her. She looked terrible—her eyes puffy, her sallow face deeply lined—but I noticed that she'd put on her one decent dress, black serge, shiny at the seams, the beautiful lace trim on the sleeves and neckline yellowed with age. It was the dress she always wore to our dance examinations, and whenever she wore it—for luck, she said— she told us about her family's lace-making business near Bruges.

"You're coming, then?"

"*Bien sûr.* Of course."

She would lose some of her wages for taking time off from the laundry, but Maman had always made it a point to accompany us to our examinations. She sat with the other mothers in the stalls behind the orchestra pit—seats usually reserved for the gentleman subscribers, some of whom also attended the examinations. These were the only times Maman saw us dance, and it pleased her to sit next to a wealthy *abonné*.

"You'll do well today, Marie," she said. "You always do. You make me proud."

I glanced at her. So much of the time I was angry at my mother, but there were moments like this when I truly felt that she loved me.

We drank our bitter coffee in silence, listening to the tick of the clock.

Charlotte was the next to wake up; as usual, it took all three of us to rouse Antoinette. We left early in order to have time to warm up before the examinations began. There was no conversation as we hurried to the Palais Garnier. Maman kissed us and gave us each a blessing before she went off to the *grande salle de spectacle;* we headed for the dressing room to change into the new practice tutus that were given out for the spring examinations.

The tension in the Palais Garnier was so high you could almost smell it, like the air before a summer thunderstorm. At each examination several dancers were found unacceptable and told not to return, bringing a painful end to all their dreams as well as to the sometimes desperate hopes of the mothers huddled anxiously in the *grande salle*. Failure meant disaster. There were no second chances.

I tried to put this out of my mind, but it was very hard. I was always fearful, not only for myself, but for my sisters as well. My friends Geneviève, Léonie, Mathilde, and I tied bright ribbons in one another's hair and wished one another luck, although we knew the luck we wanted most was for ourselves.

I tried not to think too much, not to worry, to keep myself calm and let my body do what it had been training to do for so long. We trooped to the practice rooms to warm up, and Madame Théodore, whispering *"Bonne chance"*—good luck—gave out paper numbers to be pinned to our bodices, front and back, to help the judges identify us. I was number eighteen. She led us to the area in the *coulisses* where we would wait our turn, and then she and Monsieur Dufresne, the violinist, took their places at the side of the stage. At precisely 9:30 the examinations began with the *classe des petites*, the youngest dancers. Charlotte was in this group.

A trio of *rats* in little gray slippers—they were still too young for *pointe* shoes—nervously stepped onto the stage. The violinist played a few bars to set the adagio tempo, and at the signal the little dancers carefully executed the eleven basic positions of the body as Madame Théodore called them out: *"Effacé* front! *Attitude* in *effacé*! *Écarté* back! *Développé* in that position!"

At another signal the tempo of the music increased, and the girls repeated the same basic positions in different variations at a much higher speed. When they finished, three more dancers took their places while the judges scribbled hasty notes. One child lost her balance, got out of step with the others, and rushed off the stage in tears. Charlotte never faltered. Her steps were always cleanly executed, quick without seeming hurried. Best of all, she looked happy: While some of the other girls frowned in concentration, Charlotte beamed with pleasure.

The morning crawled by. I retied my slippers and tried to concentrate on keeping my muscles warm and relaxed. At last the *premier quadrille* was called. We were examined on our jumps and turns, both fast and slow, with special attention to *port de bras,* the position of the arms. I was a little off-balance on one of my landings—had the judges noticed? Would that count against me?

As I left the stage, chewing my lip, worried about my fate, I saw Monsieur Degas in the wings, with his sketchbook. He was drawing Antoinette as she adjusted her tights, but when he noticed me, he stopped—pencil hovering above the paper—and gazed at me as though he were about to speak. Then it was Antoinette's turn to go onstage, and the artist turned and walked away, saying nothing.

MAMAN WAS WAITING for us outside. My sisters, my friends, and I had all passed, although one of Antoinette's friends had been dismissed for having too many absences. Best of all, Charlotte had advanced to the *classe des grandes.* We were giddy with relief, but Charlotte was weeping for her friend Amélie, the little girl who'd lost her balance and been dismissed.

"You should be happy it wasn't you," said Antoinette. "Always be happy when it's someone else and not you."

Our mother proposed that we have a meal at le Rat Mort to celebrate. A fine idea—omelets, bread, cheese, coffee—

but once we'd ordered Maman discovered that she had no money.

"I was certain that I'd brought a franc or two with me," she murmured, pretending to search in her worn purse. Antoinette watched, tapping her fingers on the table until she lost patience.

"Never mind, Maman," she said brusquely. "I'll pay."

8

Thirteen Avenue Trudaine

On Tuesdays and Thursdays after rehearsals I stopped at the laundry to pick up Monsieur Degas's clean linens, left them with Madame Sabine, and then climbed the stairs to the studio. He was always waiting, impatient to begin, irritated if I came even a little late.

"*Bonjour, ma petite.*" He called me "little one" or "my girl" or "mademoiselle," but rarely by my name. I sometimes wondered if he even remembered my name. Maybe all his models were the same to him.

"*Bonjour,* Monsieur Degas," I would reply.

I always undressed quickly, without any of the earlier embarrassment. I tried to please him, to find the pose quickly and to hold it without moving, until he released me. As daylight faded, or if the day was gloomy, he would light a lamp and keep working.

In the beginning I was reluctant to ask for a break unless Monsieur Degas offered it—*"Alors,* time for a little rest?"—although he usually seemed solicitous of my comfort, asking me if I felt cold. Once he gave me an orange and showed me how to peel it without damaging the flesh, making a long, curling spiral of rind. I ate it greedily, the juices running down my chin, and thought I had never tasted anything so delicious.

At the end of the three hours I left with one franc fifty in my pocket.

Sometimes when I arrived at Monsieur Degas's studio, he had visitors—other artists who came to talk about art, to complain about the galleries that had rejected them, or to discuss plans to organize an exhibition of their work themselves. I half listened to their conversations while I undressed behind the screen, waiting until they were gone before I stepped out.

Each time I wondered if Mademoiselle Cassatt might come by again. I would have felt embarrassed to have her see me naked, but my shyness was balanced by my curiosity about the lady artist who wore such elegant clothes.

The weeks passed, and although the Cassatt sisters never came while I was in the studio, I knew that they had been there. Scattered across the worktable were several drawings of Mademoiselle Mary, a slender figure leaning on her furled umbrella, and of Mademoiselle Lydia, seated and peering intently at a book. Monsieur Degas had reworked the figures, moving them closer together or farther apart, sometimes reversing them so that Mademoiselle Mary leaned to the left in one picture, to the right in another. The backgrounds changed, too—to different galleries in the Louvre, where the ladies were supposed to be looking at the art. Monsieur Degas never seemed satisfied with his work; he was always changing something or starting over.

ONE WARM SPRING DAY, as I stepped through the door of Monsieur Degas's studio, a small dog with wiry, reddish brown fur, a clownish face, and black eyes shiny as beads leaped off the divan and began yapping at me madly. I backed away. Monsieur Degas ordered the dog to be quiet and was at first ignored, but finally the barking subsided to a low growl.

"I didn't know you had a dog," I said uneasily.

"This wretched animal does not belong to me," Monsieur Degas explained. "He belongs to Mademoiselle Cassatt. I'm merely allowing him to stay here for a few days while his mistress is away from Paris. Today, I'm happy to say, is his last day as my guest. I'm to escort him to his home later this evening."

The little dog retreated to its place among the pillows on the divan, where it regarded me suspiciously. I reached a hand tentatively toward the dog's short black nose. It woofed softly, low in its throat, but allowed me to pat its head.

"Does it have a name?" I asked.

"Possibly. I haven't bothered to inquire. Such a useless creature," grumbled Monsieur Degas. "Why anyone would want to put up with a dog is beyond my comprehension. Now, a horse is an entirely different matter. Wouldn't you agree that a horse is a beautiful animal, elegant as well as useful, compared to this worthless bundle of noise and fur?"

"*Oui*, I agree that horses are beautiful, but I think they eat a great deal." The little dog licked my hand with its tiny pink tongue. We were becoming friends.

"Then there is the matter of manure," added Monsieur Degas, with a loud bark of laughter.

We joked about the relative merits of dogs and horses, until he said, "*Eh bien,* my girl, let's get to work."

I undressed and stepped up onto the model's stand. "The usual pose, Monsieur?" I asked.

"*Oui, oui.*" He was bent over the table, studying his earlier drawings of my feet, my hands, my face.

I took the pose with my feet in fourth position. I no longer shrank from him when he touched me to make some adjustment. He seemed to have made up his mind that my hands should be clasped behind my back, fingers laced, chin lifted. The pose wasn't difficult to assume, although the tension in my shoulders still made it hard to hold the pose for long.

That day he had me turn and face the wall. I studied a brownish stain on the plaster near the ceiling. After a few minutes I could hear him humming a tune under his breath.

"Monsieur Degas, what is that pretty song?" I asked.

"A folk tune from an old French comic opera," he said, proceeding to sing it aloud. "Now repeat after me: *'Robin m'aime, Robin m'a.'*"

I protested, "But, Monsieur, I can't sing."

"Of course you can," he growled. "Everyone can sing. Now, let's hear you: *'Robin m'aime, Robin m'a.'*"

Feeling foolish, I did, repeating the song, line for line, until I had learned both words and tune. How strange it was, standing naked, facing a wall, singing with Monsieur Degas while he drew. I have never forgotten that song—I can remember it to this day.

> *Robin loves me, I am his,*
> *Robin wants to marry me,*
> *Then he'll be mine.*

At the end of the session, as Monsieur Degas was counting out the coins into my palm, he was suddenly struck by an idea. "Listen, *ma petite*," he said, "is it possible that you could do me an immense favor?"

"*Oui*, Monsieur. What is it?"

"The miserable dog," he said. The dog, which had settled into a nap on the divan, seemed to know it was being talked about and was immediately on guard, ears pricked, eyes darting. "He is to go home this evening to his mistress, and I was requested to take him there. But I'm already late for an appointment. Would you be so kind as to deliver him to Mademoiselle Cassatt for me? She lives not far from here. I'll pay you for your trouble, of course."

I would have gladly done the errand for nothing, but Monsieur Degas insisted, dropping an additional fifty centimes into my hand. "Thirteen Avenue Trudaine," he said. "Ring the bell marked 'Cassatt.'" He printed the name on a slip of paper, folded it, and gave it to me.

"Will he follow me?" I asked. The dog was looking up at us doubtfully, head cocked to one side.

"*Non*. He is completely spoiled, worse than any child. You must carry him down the stairs, but then he will go along nicely on his leash."

I tucked the dog under my arm. Once we reached the street and I'd set him on the pavement, he trotted along briskly, bursting with his own importance, pausing every few meters to sniff and leave his mark, and stopping at 13 Avenue Trudaine. It was a handsome stone building with marble carvings surrounding the entrance, and tall double doors that opened into an atrium filled with light pouring from a skylight. The porter, a ruddy-faced man in a blue smock, poked his head out of his cubbyhole under the stairs. The dog yapped at him in a familiar way.

"Ah, Batty!" said the porter, stooping with his hands on

his knees so that his face was close to the dog's. "You've come home again!"

So that was the dog's name: Batty.

The porter pointed out a small brass plate engraved CASSATT and pressed the bell next to it. A tinny voice came out of a speaking tube, asking my name. I shouted into the tube that I had come from Monsieur Degas's studio and had Batty with me, to deliver to Mademoiselle Cassatt. The tinny voice instructed me to come to the fifth floor.

With the little dog again under my arm, I climbed to the Cassatt apartment. A maid in a neat black uniform with a collar of white linen opened the door. Her face changed expression, as though she expected to find one of Mademoiselle Cassatt's artist friends on the doorstep, not a skinny girl in ragged clothes.

Batty wriggled to be let down, but I held him fast and told the maid that I must speak to Mademoiselle Mary Cassatt. "Tell her that Marie van Goethem is here, *je vous en prie*—I beg you. I assure you that she will recognize my name at once."

"Mademoiselle Mary isn't at home," she said—smugly, I thought, as though the uniform gave her importance. "She and Mademoiselle Lydia have gone out."

I had no choice but to hand over Batty, who seemed overjoyed to be home again. Disappointed not to have seen Mademoiselle Cassatt, I descended the flights of stairs slowly, trailing my hand along the iron railing, round and round at each landing, until I reached the street.

Twilight crept over the city, turning the pale sky to lavender, and the air was warm and sweet. Nearby in Place d'Anvers, people strolled beneath the leafy young trees, among bushes nearly smothered with bright flowers. Although my home lay in the opposite direction, I lingered in the park—a much more pleasant place.

From a bench I watched passersby come and go, on foot and in carriages, my thoughts drifting dreamily. After a while, as the lavender sky deepened to purple, I left Place d'Anvers and began to walk slowly toward Rue de Douai. But on the way, just as I had nearly passed 13 Avenue Trudaine, a smart-looking carriage rolled to a stop by the entrance. The coachman jumped down from his seat, tied the handsome chestnut mare to a hitching post, and hurried to open the carriage door.

The first to emerge was Mademoiselle Mary Cassatt, and she and the coachman both turned to help Mademoiselle Lydia. The two ladies, fussing with their purses and hatboxes and bundles, appeared not to notice me, but the coachman did. For a moment we stared at each other.

I immediately recognized Jean-Pierre Bordenave, who'd been our neighbor when we were children. Soon after my father's death, my mother had moved us stealthily, in the middle of the night, to avoid the rent collector; she'd done it twice more since then for the same reason, always to a meaner place than the one we'd just left. Although we hadn't seen each other in several years, Jean-Pierre recognized me, too, and touched the brim of his top hat in greeting.

That attracted the notice of Mademoiselle Lydia, who frowned at him and said sharply, "Jean-Pierre, we'd be most grateful if you could be of some assistance."

Mademoiselle Mary turned to investigate the source of her sister's complaint and saw me, poised uneasily, not sure whether to stay or to flee. "*Eh bien,* it's Monsieur Degas's little dancer! What are you doing here, Marie?"

"I've just returned Batty," I explained, flushing with embarrassment. I had wanted so much to see her, but now that she was here, I was nearly tongue-tied. "At the request of Monsieur Degas."

"That was kind of you, Marie. And was he well behaved?"

"Monsieur Degas is always well behaved, Mademoiselle," I replied sincerely. I realized my mistake too late, but it sent both Cassatt sisters into peals of merry laughter.

Loaded down with parcels, Jean-Pierre managed to open the door to the atrium and stepped aside for the Cassatts to enter. "Wait here," he whispered to me, preparing to follow the sisters inside.

While I waited for Jean-Pierre, I stroked the carriage horse's rough mane. When Jean-Pierre and I were children, we'd shared secrets and dreams, although he was two years older. We'd played in the street together, and he'd pranced around on a broomstick, pretending to be riding a horse. He'd dreamed that someday he would become a jockey and would ride in the races at Longchamp. But now he was nearly a man, already too tall to be a jockey. Instead he was dressed in coachman's livery.

Jean-Pierre was back sooner than I expected, having turned the ladies' parcels over to the ruddy-faced porter. He smiled broadly and removed his top hat, revealing an unruly crop of yellow curls.

"Don't let the fancy hat fool you," he said. "I work for the stable where the old gentleman boards his carriage horse and the young lady keeps her riding horse," he explained. "I spend most of my time shoveling manure when I'm not driving the ladies around Paris. You know them?"

I explained that I was a dancer and, now, a model posing for the artist, Monsieur Degas. "The Cassatt ladies come to visit at his studio," I added.

Jean-Pierre looked at me thoughtfully. "I must take the carriage back to the stable. I can leave you off on the way."

I had never in my life ridden in a carriage. "But won't they object?" I asked.

"Meet me at the next corner. They won't object if they don't know." He swung up onto the coachman's seat, flicked the whip over the back of the chestnut mare, and drove off.

In case the porter happened to be watching, I crossed the street and walked off briskly toward the corner where Jean-Pierre was waiting. He helped me into the carriage, although

I needed no help, and I settled back onto the leather seat, feeling like a grand lady indeed.

"Where to, Mademoiselle?" he asked over his shoulder.

"Four Rue Frochot, *s'il vous plaît*," I called, ashamed to give him my own shabby address. I had given him Monsieur Degas's instead.

The carriage rolled to a stop in front of the narrow door with the chipped green paint, and I stepped down to the street before the coachman could spring from his seat to assist. *"Merci,"* I said. *"Au revoir,"* I added quickly, eager for him to be gone before he realized that I didn't live at this address.

"À bientôt," said Jean-Pierre, smiling broadly. "See you soon."

"Oui, see you soon."

I turned away, pretending to search for a key until I heard the carriage clatter away. Then I hurried home, wondering if I *would* see him again. Perhaps it had been wrong to give him Monsieur Degas's address—another of those little lies that might someday catch up with me.

9

Jean-Pierre

One warm day in June I knocked on the door of Monsieur Degas's studio, as I had more than a dozen times before. He looked startled when he peered out and found me standing there.

"Ah, Mademoiselle," he said. "What a pleasant surprise."

"Surprise? But I always come at this time." I stepped inside, thinking that he probably had guests—the Cassatt ladies, perhaps—and had forgotten. But I saw at once that he was alone. Then I noticed on his worktable a small figure made of looped and twisted wire: a dancer in fourth position, hands behind her back, head tilted. I recognized her at a glance: *me!* I took a step toward it. "Is that it? The statuette?"

"*Non, non,*" he said, "only a maquette—a sketch, as it were. The sculpture itself will be much larger. About so high." He held his hand at the level of his waist.

"May I look?"

"Ah, *oui.*" Monsieur Degas bowed and stepped aside.

I approached the wire figure cautiously, examining it from all sides. "The wires—they're like the lines in a drawing, aren't they? It's simple, but it shows so much."

Monsieur Degas smiled. "I'm glad you see it so clearly. But this is only the beginning. An experiment. There's much more to be done. Still, if all goes well, I'll enter the finished statuette in an exhibit next spring."

For a moment we gazed at the figure together, tenderly.

"Shall I undress?" I asked when he'd said nothing more.

"Undress?" Again, the startled look. "Ah, I must have neglected to tell you last time," he said. "For several months I'll be working from the drawings to finish the maquette, but I'll send for you again when the final sculpture is under way. Agreed? You'll come back when I need you?"

"*Bien sûr*—of course, Monsieur," I said in a low voice, trying to hide my disappointment. He had no way of knowing how important this work was for me, how desperately I needed the money.

"I'll be away much of the summer," he explained, "visiting friends in the country. The Cassatts. Others, too. Paris in the summer is insufferable, as you know."

"*Oui,*" I said. "I know." As though I, too, could leave for a summer holiday in the country if I wished!

"See here," he muttered gruffly, digging in his pocket, "I'll pay you for today, even though you did no work, and for next week as well. That's fair, isn't it?"

"*Oui, merci,*" I said, brushing away the tears that had gathered in my eyes.

Monsieur Degas dropped more coins into my hand than I think he first intended. They were the last I would see for some time, I knew. I fled down the stairs, clutching the coins. No doubt he had forgotten about me before I even reached the street.

Somehow I had come to believe that I would always be Monsieur Degas's model, continuing to visit the studio once or twice a week and coming away with one franc fifty each time, until the sculpture was finished. The work was far from completed. Not until he'd twisted wire into a form no bigger than a doll did I recognize anything that resembled a statuette.

Had he seen the disappointment in my eyes? I could hardly disguise it, but then he'd paid little attention all along to the Marie that was not part of his art.

Before going up to our rooms, I stopped in at the tobacconist's shop on the ground floor of our building. Monsieur Lerat, the lumbering, shaggy-haired owner, who reminded me of a great, friendly bear, set down his pipe and smiled.

"*Eh bien,* Marie, another deposit for the bank?" he asked, reaching under the counter for the tarnished tin in which he and his wife kept my money safe for me.

"*Oui,* but the last one for some time," I said. "My modeling job is finished for the present."

He clucked his tongue—*tch tch!*—and shook his head. "*C'est dommage,*" he said. "A pity. But surely another artist will be happy to hire a lovely girl like you."

I opened the tin and dumped the coins out onto the counter: six francs, plus half of what Monsieur Degas had paid me that day; the rest I would give to Maman. "Come now, *ma petite,*" the tobacconist called after me as I left his shop. "Things are sure to get better."

"*Peut-être,*" I allowed. "Maybe."

MY LIFE CONTINUED as it had before I met Monsieur Degas: morning classes, afternoon rehearsals, errands for Maman, evening performances at the Opéra. Sometimes Monsieur Degas sat in his usual place with his drawing pad. He'd said he was going to the country—why, then, was he still here? Had he found another girl to pose for him? I was immediately jealous of her, whoever she was. He seldom spoke to me or even gave the slightest sign that he knew me. That angered me, and I vowed that if he *did* speak to me, I would look straight through him as though he didn't exist.

Sometimes he didn't appear for days on end, and I wondered if he'd gone away. I missed the hours I used to spend in his studio. During those hours I'd felt as though I mattered mattered enough that a great artist like Monsieur Degas wanted to make a sculpture of me. Not just a picture, but a statue! That showed I was of some importance to someone. Now I was of little importance to anyone.

The first to notice my dreary mood was Madame Théodore, who called me aside one day after a rehearsal of *La sylphide*, in which I danced as one of the bridesmaids. "Marie, what ails you? Are you ill?"

"*Non,* Madame."

"What's wrong, then? Because you dance as though you were carrying a sack of oats on your back and a horseshoe in each hand."

"Nothing is wrong, Madame," I said. I couldn't meet her steady gaze—it was as though she were looking into my soul—and I stared at the floor.

"A dancer cannot allow her private feelings to dictate her dancing. She must dance the dance, whether her heart is bursting with joy or breaking with sadness. Do you understand, Marie?"

"*Oui,* Madame," I murmured. "I understand." And I did.

THAT NIGHT in our performance of *La sylphide* I somehow moved too close to a *premier sujet* who was dancing the solo role of Old Madge, the sorceress. Moments later, offstage in the *coulisses,* she brought down her wrath even before the *étoile* dancing the Sylphide had finished her *révérences* to the audience.

"Pay attention, you stupid, clumsy girl," the *sujet* snarled, pushing past me. I would have pushed her back had my friend Mathilde not stepped between us.

I was in a foul humor as I rushed away from the Palais Garnier after the performance, not even noticing that Jean-Pierre Bordenave stood waiting outside. "Marie!" he called, running to catch up with me. "I'm going to see the electric lights on Place de l'Opéra. Will you come with me?"

I had thought often of Jean-Pierre since he'd driven me in the Cassatts' carriage, and I was pleased to see him, but all I really wanted then was to go home. Nevertheless, I agreed to go with him.

Electric lights had just been installed all along Avenue de l'Opéra, replacing the gas lamps, and that night they were to be turned on for the first time in honor of the opening of the Paris Universal Exposition. Together we gazed at the awesome spectacle: Place de l'Opéra was flooded with brilliant light; the entire area around the Palais Garnier was nearly as bright as daylight—as though night had been banished. But the spectacle did little to dispel my bleak mood.

"The electric lights were just an excuse," said Jean-Pierre. "To be honest, Marie, I came to walk home with you."

I was too tired and dispirited to say much as we trudged up Rue Pigalle, but Jean-Pierre was not at a loss for words.

"The Cassatts have gone away for the summer," he said. "They've rented a house in the country and taken the train there. I'm not needed for driving, but I'm to care for the horses until the ladies come back in September."

"And the dog?" I asked. "Has he gone with them?"

"*Bien sûr.* You know Batty, then? The silly dog goes everywhere. The Cassatts are American, did you know that?"

"That explains their odd accent," I said.

"Their brother came from America recently with his family for a visit. I've driven them a time or two. They're very rich. That is, the brother is."

"The sisters as well, I imagine," I said. "Their clothes look very expensive."

"I'm going to America someday," Jean-Pierre continued, naming the cities he planned to visit: New York, Chicago, San Francisco. "And I've heard that some people in New Orleans speak French." I listened quietly. Such dreams he had!

We were nearing Rue de Douai. "Shall we have coffee, Marie?" Jean-Pierre asked. "Would you like something to eat? We could go to le Rat Mort. It's close by."

How nice it would be, I thought, *to sit at le Rat Mort with Jean-Pierre, sipping coffee or eating an ice cream.* But suppose my mother was there, groggy with drink, or my sister Antoinette with her gentleman from the *foyer de la danse.* I turned away. "*Non, non merci.* I must go home. My younger sister . . ."

"Maybe some other time, then?" Jean-Pierre took my hand as we stopped beneath a streetlamp. I couldn't help noticing how good-looking he had become, his curls gleaming like gold in the yellow gaslight.

"*Oui,* another time." But I'd begun to worry that he would find out that I had lied and would see where I actually lived—in an ugly, run-down building on a street of ugly, run-down buildings. There was so much in my life that I was ashamed of. "*Bonne nuit,* Jean-Pierre," I said, forcing a smile. "Good night. I must go. I'll find my way from here." I tried to pull my hand away from his, but he clasped it tighter.

"Marie," he said. "Listen to me: I want to be friends again, the way we used to be."

We stood in a circle of lamplight, our fingers laced.

"Of course," I said. "We can be friends."

"Then come with me on Sunday to the Bois de Boulogne. Would you like that?"

I had only been to the Bois, a park on the outskirts of Paris, a few times, before my father fell ill. "*Oui,*" I said, "I would." I thought quickly. "I'll meet you at noon at Place Blanche."

"Promise?"

"I promise." This time my smile came readily, and it was real.

10

The Bois de Boulogne

Antoinette slept late on Sunday, stretched languidly, and began preparing to go out with her friends, while I fidgeted nervously.

"Come with us, Marie! We're going to the Universal Exposition. Everyone's raving about it. I'll lend you a franc or two. We'll have a jolly time."

I refused, explaining that I had other things to do.

She studied me closely. "You could do with some gaiety in your life, little sister," she said. "Your face looks pinched."

I shrugged and turned away. "I'm all right," I said.

As soon as she'd gone tripping down the stairs—in a new dress of rose mousseline, cut very low in the bosom—I opened the wardrobe and examined her dresses; I finally chose a green silk faille trimmed with pleated ruching and black lace. It fit me poorly, but I had no time to do more than cinch in the waist sash and tuck up the hem with a few pins. I tied the strings of the matching green bonnet under my chin, stuffed bits of cotton wool into the toes of her second-best leather boots—which were also too large—and rummaged through her wooden trunk until I found a pair of lavender gloves and an embroidered handkerchief, on which I dabbed a few drops of her scent.

Charlotte, seated cross-legged on the bed, chin cradled in her hands, had been watching me with solemn eyes. "Where are you going, Marie?" she asked.

"To meet my friend Jean-Pierre. He was our neighbor long ago, before Papa died."

"I remember him, I think," she said wistfully.

It was close to noon, and I was nearly ready. "Where's Maman?" I asked from the depths of the wardrobe, where I was searching for a parasol.

"She went out. She didn't say where, or when she was coming back." Charlotte sighed.

I hesitated, but only for a moment. "Put on your best dress," I said, emerging with a white lace parasol, "and come with me." I opened the parasol and twirled it. The wooden handle was missing, but it would do nicely. "Hurry," I said.

Charlotte brightened and sprang off the bed. Back we plunged into the wardrobe, to find her a skirt and a chemise and a pretty little shawl. Her old sabots would have to do.

On our way out I stopped at the tobacconist's shop and withdrew three fifty-centime pieces from my "bank."

"You look so pretty," said Monsieur Lerat, watching me knot the coins in the corner of the handkerchief. "You must be going out with your sweetheart."

I blushed. "I don't have a sweetheart."

"*Alors là,* you should!" The tobacconist winked at me. "Enjoy yourself, Marie."

IF JEAN-PIERRE was surprised that I had brought my young sister, he gave no sign. In fact, he looked truly pleased to see Charlotte, grinning broadly—that splendid smile of his!—and bowing low over her hand. He was dressed in what must have been his Sunday best, although it was ill fitting, the trouser legs stopping short of his ankles and the jacket sleeves exposing his wrists. But his shirt was very white, a blue necktie was knotted loosely around his neck in the current fashion, and his cap seemed to be new. I was glad I'd taken the trouble to dress nicely in my borrowed finery.

We boarded a yellow omnibus drawn by six draft horses and already filled with families eager to escape the heat of Paris. At each stop more passengers crowded aboard until we could scarcely breathe, the ladies' skirts all crushed together with no room left even to flutter a fan. A little breeze slipped in through the open sides of the omnibus, fortunately, or I think we might have suffocated. At last we reached the old fortification surrounding the city, passed through the Porte Maillot, and entered the Bois de Boulogne.

Many on board were on their way to the Longchamp racecourse. However, we climbed down when we reached the Porte Dauphine, and followed a meandering gravel path. Charlotte skipped on ahead, eager to be the first to glimpse the lake.

The water was smooth as a mirror, reflecting the tree branches that overhung its banks. Men in straw hats rowed small boats in idle circles. On the terraces of cafés and restaurants beside the lake, waiters in long white aprons balanced trays high above their heads and threaded their way among the crowded tables. A juggler performed on the lawn, and hawkers sold ices and sweets from little wheeled carts.

Antoinette's heavy silk dress proved much too warm for the day; perspiration trickled down my back, and I dabbed at my face with the free corner of the handkerchief. Her boots had begun to pinch and rub, and I was relieved when we found a vacant bench in the shade and sat down to rest. Jean-Pierre bought a bottle of cider from a toothless old woman with a gaily painted cart, and produced from his knapsack a loaf of bread, a round of cheese, a sausage laced with garlic, and two ripe pears—only two, because he hadn't expected Charlotte. He carefully divided everything three ways, making sure that my sister and I always got the larger portions. He pretended not to notice how ravenously we devoured this magnificent feast.

Charlotte saved some bread crumbs to toss to the ducks paddling busily among the rushes at the edge of the lake, while Jean-Pierre entertained me with stories of the horses at the livery stable and asked me questions about Monsieur Degas.

"Does he treat you respectfully, Marie?" he asked. "I've heard that artists sometimes take liberties with their models."

I assured him that Monsieur Degas always behaved honorably. "But there's no need for concern. I'm no longer modeling for him. My work there is finished, at least for the present."

When her supply of crumbs was exhausted, my sister grew restless. I was annoyed when she asked Jean-Pierre, "Might we rent a boat for just a short while?"

"Charlotte!" I said sharply, for I felt that Jean-Pierre had already done a great deal for us. "You know we have no money for such things."

"But you got some from Monsieur Lerat," she reminded me, her eyes wide.

Jean-Pierre laughed. "I'll go and ask about a boat," he promised, "if you'll tell me about this Monsieur Lerat who gives you money."

"The tobacconist in our building keeps my money for me in a tin," I explained. I untied the coins in my handkerchief and offered them to Jean-Pierre to help pay for the boat, but he refused and set off at a run along the path for the pier where boats were tied up.

Soon he trotted back to inform us that he had hired a skiff for a half hour, the minimum time allowed. Within minutes we had climbed down from the wooden pier and settled ourselves into a small boat, Charlotte at the stern and I at the bow. Jean-Pierre, seated in the middle with the oars, began to row toward the center of the lake. I leaned back and trailed my fingers in the cool water as I had seen other ladies do, Antoinette's lace parasol tilted on my shoulder, the strings of her bonnet undone. What a charming picture we must have made! I closed my eyes and turned my face up to the sun.

I'm not sure exactly what happened next. Maybe I drifted off in a half slumber, but somehow I let go of the parasol, which fell into the water. I woke up with a start and reached out to snatch it back just as Charlotte also leaned over to rescue the parasol. The skiff tipped. Charlotte was the first to topple into the water. Jean-Pierre leaped in after her. I, scrambling to somehow save them, followed the others. None of us knew how to swim.

My skirts billowed up around me. The boat bobbed just out of reach, but I managed to seize an oar and held it out toward Jean-Pierre, who had got hold of the flailing, screaming Charlotte. By some miracle, two or three other boaters had seen our predicament and raced to our aid, and several brave gentlemen sacrificed their Sunday finery by jumping into the water and keeping us afloat.

Eventually we all made our way to shore, coughing and badly frightened, our clothes a sodden mess. The parasol had disappeared beneath the murky surface, and one lavender glove was missing. Jean-Pierre had lost his new cap. The bonnet, fished out by one of our rescuers, appeared to be ruined, and Antoinette's green silk dress had suffered several rips and tears, and was now the color of mud. Charlotte sobbed inconsolably, and I was sick with worry. Only Jean-Pierre seemed unperturbed. He had managed to push the skiff to shore. Now he clambered into it and rowed it back to the pier.

When Jean-Pierre returned, he spread his jacket on the grass for me, removed his necktie, and stretched out in the warm sunshine. Following his example I pulled off the borrowed boots, although I didn't dare to roll down my stockings. I unfastened my braid and allowed Charlotte to comb out my wet hair.

Charlotte noticed a little medal gleaming in the opening of Jean-Pierre's mud-streaked shirt. "What is it?" she asked him.

"Saint Christophe, the patron of travelers. My mother gave it to me. It's the most valuable thing I own."

"Is it real gold?"

"Charlotte," I said in a warning voice.

"Maybe. But that's not why it's valuable. It protects me from accidents."

"But it didn't keep the boat from tipping over," Charlotte pointed out.

"*Non*, but we were rescued, weren't we?"

Our clothes were mostly dry when we boarded an omnibus for the trip back to the city a few hours later, but passengers returning from the racecourse stared at my torn and mud-stained dress and ruined bonnet. Antoinette was always careful of her belongings, jealously guarding them and unwilling to lend out even a pair of stockings, so I was afraid of how she would react when she discovered what had happened to her green silk dress. I tried to think of what I would tell her, but by the time we reached the city I still had no idea.

"I was going to suggest that next week we visit the Canal Saint-Martin," Jean-Pierre joked as we parted in Place Blanche, "but I think you've both had enough of the water for a while." Then he added, "I will see you again soon, I hope?"

Before I could answer, Charlotte cried out a little too enthusiastically, "*Mais oui,* Jean-Pierre! We'd love to!"

"*Très bien,*" he said. "Very good. And you, Marie? What's your answer?"

"*Moi, aussi,*" I replied, pleased at the idea. "Me, too." If he was disappointed that he would again be seeing two Van Goethem sisters instead of one, he hid it well.

"Then give me your boots as a pledge," he said, looking down at Antoinette's boots, much the worse for their soaking. "Neat's-foot oil will make them good as new. You'll see."

I pulled off the damp boots and handed them over to Jean-Pierre, and we agreed to meet the following Sunday at the Café de la Nouvelle-Athènes, near Place Pigalle. "Eight o'clock," he said. "The boots will be ready."

As Charlotte and I hurried home, the pavement gritty under my stocking feet, I finally worked out a plan, which I explained to Charlotte: We would take the ruined dress to Tante Hélène's workroom and ask her to help fix it—the bonnet, too. With luck, Antoinette would likely not miss her parasol or her one lavender glove, or look for her old boots before next week. The plan was desperate and depended heavily on Tante Hélène, but I could think of nothing better.

AT HOME I changed clothes quickly, wrapped Antoinette's muddy dress and bonnet in my tartan shawl, and hid the bundle at the bottom of my wooden trunk.

When Antoinette returned that evening from her visit to the Universal Exposition, she could talk of nothing else. "Tourists are coming from everywhere to see it. You can't travel anywhere in the city in peace. We stood in line for over an hour to climb up inside the head and shoulders of an enormous statue. It's called *Liberty Enlightening the World*, and from the top you can see all over Paris. When it's finished it's to be shipped to America." I held my breath while she kicked off her good boots and undressed. "What did you two do today?" she asked.

Charlotte and I looked at each other. "Nothing," we said.

That night, after Antoinette had fallen asleep, Charlotte whispered, "Is Jean-Pierre your sweetheart?"

"Don't be foolish," I said. "I have no sweetheart. Besides, we nearly drowned him."

11

A Green Silk Dress

harlotte met me at the Palais Garnier, after my rehearsal, with the bundle containing Antoinette's ruined dress. Together we went off in search of our aunt's workroom on *la rive gauche*. I had been there two or three times with Papa and thought I could find the way.

We walked along Avenue de l'Opéra toward the Seine, passed the Louvre, and crossed the river by way of the Pont Neuf. Once we'd reached *la rive gauche*, the Left Bank, we found our way to the Passage du Pont-Neuf, tucked away at the end of the Rue Guénégaud. Even on such a bright day the narrow passageway remained gloomy and damp. The moss-covered stone walls were pockmarked with age and as dreary as those on Rue de Douai. When we thought we'd found the right building, we climbed a crooked stairway to a dimly lit landing and knocked on a door painted with the silhouette of a dressmaker's dummy.

The door whisked open, and Tante Hélène's heavy eyebrows lifted in surprise to find the two of us on her threshold. "Come in, come in, my girls!" she cried, crushing us to her ample bosom and kissing us each on both cheeks before she pulled us into her large workroom.

At least a dozen girls in drab gray dresses hunched over their work at long tables, their needles flying in and out of the cloth spread in front of them. Two older women were pinning paper patterns to lengths of silk and linen; others cut out the cloth with large scissors. In one corner a couple of seamstresses assembled parts of a gown on a dressmaker's dummy. They darted inquisitive glances at us but didn't slow their busy cutting and pinning and stitching.

"So, *mes petites,* to what do I owe this visit?" Tante Hélène asked heartily. "Have you come to work for me, as I've been begging you for so long?"

Never, I thought, but I kept my thoughts to myself and hurried to explain the nature of our errand. "We've brought a dress that got torn in a few places. We came to see if you could fix it. I'll pay you for it," I added. "I've saved a little money."

Charlotte placed the bundle on the table and undid the knotted shawl. Tante Hélène lifted up the damaged dress, which looked even worse after having been buried in my trunk. *"Zut!"* she exclaimed. "And how did this dress fall into such a sorry state?"

I had tried to think of a reasonable story to explain it, but in the end I settled on the truth: that I had borrowed the dress and bonnet from Antoinette, worn them to the Bois, and tumbled into the lake. "I hope it's not ruined," I said as Tante Hélène continued to examine the unfortunate dress.

"I fell in, too," Charlotte said, her eyes innocent. "We're lucky to be alive. We can't swim," she added in a bid for our aunt's sympathy.

"Thanks be to God that you're both safe," Tante Hélène said, making the sign of the cross. "And was Antoinette with you? Did she fall in as well?"

We shook our heads.

"And does she know about the dress?"

We shook our heads again.

"I see." Her lips pursed, our aunt noted the mud stains, the rent sleeve, the torn ruching, the ripped flounces, and the ragged hem.

"All right," she sighed at last. "I'll see what I can do."

"It can be fixed, then?"

"Not perfectly, but I believe well enough. Come back to see me in a week."

"A week!" I wailed. "Antoinette is sure to find out before then!"

"*Eh bien,* you naughty girls, come on Friday, then."

"*Merci, merci!*" we cried, hugging and kissing our aunt, and away we hurried, well pleased with our errand.

ON THE WAY HOME I made an important discovery about Charlotte.

We stopped to examine a poster mounted on a wall at the corner of our street: a woman in a red dress and a black bonnet standing in front of the Moulin de la Galette, one of the old windmills on Montmartre that had been turned into a dance hall. The message was spelled out in ornate letters, which of course I couldn't read. But Charlotte *could*.

"It's for a dance on Sunday afternoon," Charlotte said, studying the poster. "'Everyone invited,' it says. It would be fun to go," she added wistfully. "Do you think Jean-Pierre might take us?"

"How do you know what it says?" I asked, ignoring her suggestion.

She glanced at me and then looked away. "I read it."

"You read it? But how did you learn to read?" I demanded.

"My friend Blanche is teaching me." Blanche was the daughter of the bassoonist in the orchestra at the Opéra; it was a family of some means. "Her mother comes with her to our classes and passes the time reading her newspaper. When I found out that Blanche could read it, too, I asked if she'd teach me. It's not so hard, if you put your mind to it,

Marie," she assured me. "I'm sure I can teach you, if you want to learn."

"I do," I said. "I do want to learn." *Reading could be a useful skill,* I thought. And how impressed Monsieur Degas and Mademoiselle Cassatt would be when they came back in the autumn and I showed them that I could read!

My lessons began that day. I found it a struggle, but Charlotte was a patient tutor. First she taught me the letters and showed me how the letters fit together to form words. She pointed to a sign above the door of the tobacconist's shop; I spelled out *t-a-b-a-c: tabac.* My first word—*tobacco*! A few doors down the street I studied the baker's window— *p-a-i-n: pain. Bread!* How wonderful! How exciting! In the next few days, as we hurried to our dance classes, Charlotte used the signs in the shop windows along the way to teach me more words. I was amazed at how much I could learn just walking to the Opéra.

"Blanche has promised to show me how to write my name," she said. "As soon as I learn, I'll teach you how to write yours."

ON FRIDAY, while Charlotte was still in her class, I stopped again at the tobacconist's shop. Monsieur Lerat wasn't there, but Madame Lerat, a gaunt, ashen-faced woman with a hacking cough, emptied the last of the coins from the tin onto the counter. I swept them into my pocket without counting them and returned to Tante Hélène's workroom.

The moment Tante Hélène opened the door, I noticed that the dressmaker's dummy in the corner was wearing Antoinette's green silk dress. On its head sat her bonnet. Both dress and bonnet looked as good as new.

I approached the dummy, aware that every girl in the shop was watching, and gazed in wonder at the miracle that had taken place. The rent in the sleeve had disappeared completely, the ruching was in perfect condition, the flounces were no longer torn. Not only had all signs of damage vanished, but every trace of mud, too. The green silk faille was as fresh as a new spring leaf.

I turned to Tante Hélène, who was watching me with her hands tucked in her sleeves. "How was this possible?" I asked, mystified.

"Secrets of the trade," she said with a self-satisfied smile.

One of the seamstresses giggled. When I glanced her way, she winked.

"And the bonnet? I remember that the ribbons were frayed. These are like new."

"Ah, well, not everything can be repaired, you know. Some things must be replaced." When I continued to marvel, she confessed, "I called upon my friend the milliner, and she made you a new one. The bonnet turned out so well that I decided to make a new dress as well."

"A new dress?" My stomach knotted. That would surely cost far more money than I had. "But I can't pay you for this," I said.

Tante Hélène lifted the dress off the dummy and folded it carefully. "Don't worry, *ma petite*, I don't want your money. It was good practice for my young apprentices. But you do owe me a favor."

"*Mais oui*, Tante Hélène, whatever you wish," I said eagerly, for I was very grateful for her help.

"Come to work for me. I'll teach you to be a seamstress. You're clever, Marie—you'll learn quickly. What I wish, more than anything, is that you give up this foolish idea of being a dancer and take up a respectable trade instead."

Foolish idea? Her words struck me like a slap in the face. "But it's not a foolish idea—I *am* a dancer," I insisted. "A *good* dancer." I began to wrap the silk dress and the bonnet in my tartan shawl, anxious now to get away.

But Tante Hélène seized my wrist and pulled me into the little parlor reserved for customers. She closed the door so that the seamstresses couldn't hear. "Marie," she said sternly, "it doesn't matter if you're as graceful as a butterfly or as clumsy as an ox, it's all the same—you'll end up in the *foyer de la danse* like your sister Antoinette, with men giving you money in return for your favors. Antoinette didn't come by her green silk dress honestly—I'm sure you know that."

"But I'll never go to the *foyer de la danse*!" I cried, painfully aware that what she said about Antoinette was true.

"Of course you will. It's inevitable. Leave the Opéra, I beg you. I can even give you a decent place to stay, if you wish. It's what your father would have wanted for you—first an honest living, then marriage and children."

"How do you know what my father wanted?" I demanded. Angry tears were streaming down my face.

"He was my brother," she replied, laying her plump hands on my shoulders. "And I'm not only your aunt but your godmother. I took vows at your christening, and I promised your father before his death that I would do whatever I could to protect you. We both knew that your mother is a weak woman—she always has been. If you come work with me, I will have fulfilled my promise and done my duty."

So I was her *duty*! I broke free of my aunt's grasp. "Never!" I cried, louder than I should have. "But don't worry—I'll repay you for everything. I'll owe you no favors." I snatched up the bundle and started for the door.

"And how will you find the money to repay me, Marie?" she called after me. "The same way Antoinette finds money—in the *foyer de la danse*?"

I didn't answer, and if she said any more, I didn't hear. I bolted, slamming the door of the workshop and racing down the stairs.

Minutes later I was again on the Pont Neuf, gazing down at the gently flowing waters of the Seine. Anger, sadness, a sense that she was right about Antoinette, about Maman, and perhaps even about my future as a dancer—all of these feelings were seething inside me. Without warning they boiled over. I heaved the bundle with the green silk dress into the Seine. It floated briefly, carried along by the current. As I watched, my mouth open in a silent scream, the bundle sank beneath the surface and disappeared.

12

Guilt

How stupid! How utterly stupid of me! The dress was gone. I couldn't even bring myself to tell Charlotte what I'd done. When she asked about the dress, I lied. "It's not ready yet."

"But when?"

"I don't know. Maybe next week. There were problems."

Then on Sunday night toward eight o'clock I managed to slip out without telling anyone where I was going; I hurried to meet Jean-Pierre at the Café de la Nouvelle-Athènes. The café was crowded, the conversation at a noisy pitch. The loudest laughter came from a group of men clustered around several tables in the rear. Among them Monsieur Degas puffed calmly on his pipe.

Jean-Pierre was waiting for me at one of the marble-topped tables. After we'd ordered our coffee, he produced a clumsy package from his knapsack and unwrapped it: Antoinette's leather boots, polished and gleaming almost like new. As I admired them, Jean-Pierre asked, "Whatever happened to the green dress you took for a swim?"

I put my head in my hands and began to weep.

"Marie? What's wrong? Tell me what happened!" he begged.

"I've done something terrible," I confessed between sobs.

"I can't believe you've done anything so terrible." He leaned across the table and touched my wet cheek. "Tell me, and maybe I can help you."

So I told him the story—most, but not all, of it.

I explained that my aunt had not simply repaired the damaged dress but had sewed an entirely new one. "Even prettier than the old one," I said. "The few francs I'd saved weren't nearly enough to pay for the yards of silk and lace, let alone for the labor of the seamstresses. But Tante Hélène wouldn't accept any money. She refused to take a single *sou*."

"That was very kind of her!" Jean-Pierre exclaimed.

"It was, but she demanded a favor instead. She insists that I give up the ballet and come to work for her to learn the trade of a seamstress. She says it's what my father would have wanted."

"You refused, of course?" Jean-Pierre was sympathetic, as I expected.

But I couldn't bring myself to tell him what my aunt had said about Maman and her weakness, or about my having a "respectable" career, or about the *foyer de la danse* and the way Antoinette got her pretty dresses and her money. Those were the parts of the story I left out.

"Of course. *Never*, I told her. But then, on the way home, I got so angry and upset that I threw the dress into the Seine."

Jean-Pierre laughed at first, thinking, I suppose, that I must be joking. When he realized I wasn't, he stared at me in disbelief. "You threw the dress into the river?" he asked, his forehead knit in a puzzled frown. "The bonnet as well? But *why*, Marie?"

He looked dumbfounded, and who could blame him? How could I possibly explain it to him when I could hardly explain it to myself? And how could I expect him to understand?

"I did it because I was angry, I suppose, and I wasn't thinking clearly. I did it just to be rid of it. And now I feel terrible."

Jean-Pierre let out a low whistle. "Does Antoinette know?"

I shook my head.

"What will you tell her?"

"I don't know," I said miserably. "She'll be angry when she finds out that I took her dress and then spoiled it. But she'll be furious if she finds out that Tante Hélène made her a brand-new one, maybe even nicer than the first, and I threw it away."

"But how will she find out about the new one?"

"Tante Hélène comes to visit us every month or two. She's sure to say something to Antoinette about the dress, the whole story will come out, and then there will be an explosion of temper heard from here to Brussels. Everyone— my mother, my sister, my aunt—will be enraged at me. Not just for ruining the first dress, but even more for throwing away the second. They'll never forgive that."

"Then you must confess, Marie. One at a time, tell them what you've done. They may be angry at first, but in the end they'll forgive you." Jean-Pierre took my hand between both of his. "I know they will. How could they help it?"

We were still sitting there, Antoinette's shiny boots on the banquette between us, when Monsieur Degas strolled past our table, his cane tucked under his arm, and left the café. If he noticed me, he gave no sign.

"He walks like a duck," Jean-Pierre murmured. "Have you noticed?"

That made me smile, and for the moment I felt a little better.

CHARLOTTE KEPT asking questions. Had I picked up the dress from Tante Hélène? When would it be finished? What was happening? At first I evaded her questions, but in the end I felt compelled to tell her what I had done.

Charlotte had a way of looking at me that reminded me of Papa. "But Marie," she said solemnly, "what you did was wrong, and you must confess."

Exactly what Jean-Pierre had said. "But how can I confess? Antoinette will be furious. She'll tell Maman to beat me."

"Antoinette will be angry, but she really can't do anything," Charlotte assured me. "And Maman doesn't ever beat us—she just threatens. Maybe they won't tell Tante Hélène, and even if they do, the worst that can happen is that our aunt won't come to visit us anymore and no longer will bring us sugared almonds. But I did love those sugared almonds," she added longingly.

FOR SEVERAL WEEKS Antoinette had been in a cheerful mood. Monsieur Chevreul had moved his family to a house in the country while he stayed in the city on business, taking the train to visit his wife and children on weekends. This gave him more time during the week for my sister.

Once I scolded her: "What do you want with another woman's husband, Antoinette? Wouldn't it be better to find one of your own?"

She laughed. "That just shows what a silly goose you are, Marie! You have absolutely no idea of how to look after yourself. When I see how most men regard their lawful wives," she went on, "I'm sure I'd much rather be a mistress. Then I can have his attention and his gifts and my freedom as well."

There was no point in arguing with Antoinette. She never budged from her point of view, and she dismissed as foolish, ridiculous, childish, and naive any opinions that varied from her own.

I became increasingly uneasy about what would happen when she went looking for her green dress and bonnet. The missing parasol and lavender glove might be put down to carelessness—she had somehow misplaced them—but one doesn't simply misplace a dress and bonnet. Sooner or later she would ask me—or, worse, ask Charlotte, who could never bring herself to lie—if either of us knew what had become of them. That green dress would suddenly become her "favorite," despite not having been worn, or even looked for, for weeks on end. She would become distraught about that missing dress.

Both Jean-Pierre and Charlotte believed that confession was the best course. I knew they were right, but I kept putting it off. The time never seemed favorable. Instead I waited grimly for my crime to be discovered.

MEANWHILE, Jean-Pierre and I had fallen into the habit of long Sunday afternoon walks together. On the first of these walks, I suggested that we meet again at Place Blanche, as we had when we were going to the Bois de Boulogne. But Jean-Pierre just smiled and shook his head.

"There's no reason for you to feel ashamed of where you

live, Marie, or to feel that you must lie to me. The truth is always better. And besides, I know where you live."

He had seen through my deception. I turned away, my face burning. "How did you find out?" I whispered.

"First, I've driven Mademoiselle Mary Cassatt and her sister many times to Monsieur Degas's studio at 4 Rue Frochot. Second, I saw Charlotte on the street and asked her to point out the tobacconist's shop that you mentioned. She was happy to do that."

"Wretched child!" I complained, unable to conceal my smile. "There's no guile in her at all."

Jean-Pierre grasped my shoulders and turned me to face him. "Marie," he said, "we must promise never to lie to each other, or our friendship means nothing. Will you promise?"

I forced myself to look into his blue eyes. *"Oui,"* I said. "Only the truth."

From then on we met at the tobacconist's shop and walked together all over Paris, from Montmartre on the north side to the Latin Quarter on the Left Bank. Jean-Pierre had me show him the exact spot on the Pont Neuf from which I had thrown Antoinette's new dress into the Seine. We followed the Canal Saint-Martin from beginning to end, to watch the boats passing through the locks. We went to the grounds of the Universal Exposition to see the gigantic head of *Liberty*, although we didn't climb to the top because there was a fee and we had no money.

Each time we were together, Jean-Pierre asked, "Have you told her yet?"

Finally, after the third or fourth time, I stamped my foot impatiently and scowled. "I'll tell you when I've done it!"

Jean-Pierre pretended to ward off blows and said he would not ask again.

As THE SUMMER passed, I began to notice yet another change in Antoinette's mood. Monsieur Chevreul had decided to spend the month of August in the country with his family and would not see Antoinette again until autumn. Being apart for a while, he explained to her—and she later explained to me—would make their time together that much sweeter, and so on.

There were no performances at the Opéra during the month of August, so although we were still required to attend morning classes six days a week, we had our evenings free. "I certainly don't need Chevreul in order to enjoy myself," Antoinette announced, and she began to spend more time with her friends from the Opéra. They went to the Moulin de la Galette to dance and drink wine. They went to the Cirque Fernando to see the amazing Miss La La hanging by her teeth from a pulley rope that hauled her to the top of the high-arching dome. They took a horse-drawn cab to the music festival at the Trocadero Palace. But all of this freedom and independence was costing her money.

"I don't suppose you could lend me a franc or two?" she

asked as she got ready to go out, for the third time in a week.

"What makes you think I have any money at all?" I snapped, hoping she hadn't found out about my secret tin at the tobacconist's. The money my aunt had refused to take for the dress was back in that tin, and I guarded it jealously.

"The situation has become impossible," Antoinette complained. "You know that most of my pay goes to Maman for rent and fuel, and without Chevreul's help I have scarcely a *sou* for myself. If he's going to be so selfish, I'll have to look for a new gentleman friend at the *foyer de la danse*." She checked her little leather purse again. "You're sure you have nothing?"

"I'm sure."

SOON AFTER Monsieur Chevreul came back from the country, he invited Antoinette to attend a café concert where a popular singer was expected to perform. That was the evening she decided to wear her green silk dress. She hunted everywhere for it, becoming agitated when she couldn't find it. Grateful that Charlotte had gone out to visit her friend Blanche, who was ill, I stood by, watching anxiously as Antoinette flung clothes left and right in her frantic search. That dress was her favorite! No other dress would do! Finally, late for her appointment, she decided on the rose-colored mousseline, discovered the absence of her parasol as well, and flounced out in a very bad temper.

When Antoinette came home later, she was in a better mood, full of tales about the entertainment at the café concert. "The singer sang 'The Song of the Dog,' and we were all howling with laughter. You'll never guess who was there—Monsieur Degas, his drawing pad on his lap as always, peering up at the singer through his pince-nez while she pawed the air like a puppy! So amusing."

"And Monsieur Chevreul?" I asked.

She smiled and shook her little leather purse. It jingled with coins.

Antoinette didn't mention the missing dress, and I hoped she had forgotten about it. But I still worried about Tante Hélène and what she might say about the dress. She hadn't come to visit us since June but surely would come soon.

THE AUTUMN DANCE examinations were to take place in mid-September, and as usual our nerves were on edge and our tempers short. The day before the examinations, I happened to walk home with Antoinette. We were both feeling anxious, but for once Antoinette tried to be encouraging. "You'll do very well, Marie," she said. "You're a born dancer—I've been watching you."

The matter of the green silk dress weighed on my conscience, and now her kind words brought back all my guilty feelings. Remorse squeezed the words out of my mouth.

As we plodded up Rue Blanche, I blurted out the story. Antoinette glared at me with narrowed eyes as I described how I had borrowed the dress and bonnet and boots, but she gave way to amused chuckles when I told her about falling out of the boat. She was amazed that I had taken the dress to our aunt, and indignant at the bargain our aunt had tried to strike with me (I didn't mention that Tante Hélène had said Antoinette was immoral). And when I confessed that I had thrown the new dress in the river, she called me a few names that I won't repeat, and then burst into shrieks of raucous laughter.

"Eh bien," she said at last, when she could speak again, "let me tell you something: I never liked that dress, and that's the truth. The color was bilious! It was Monsieur Chevreul's idea—he loves green! Don't ask me why! Was the new dress the same sickening shade? In any case I'm sure it looked much better on you than it ever did on me. Now if you had taken my rose-colored dress, that would be quite another matter."

"You were wearing your rose-colored dress that day," I reminded her. "Or I might have."

"Lucky for you, *ma petite.*"

"I'm glad you're not angry," I said. "But Tante Hélène won't find this story nearly as amusing as you do when she hears about it. And I must find a way to repay her."

"She won't hear it from me, I promise you that," said Antoinette. "Another thing—that awful old tartan shawl of yours? I'll see that you get another. Something soft and pretty." She hugged me, and I felt a rush of warmth for her.

But then she turned away. "If you really intend to repay her, you'll simply have to start visiting the *foyer de la danse*. It's the only way you'll ever climb out of this hole, you know."

I said nothing. Two days later we passed our examinations without difficulty. For once Maman had money for a lunch afterward, and I put the *foyer de la danse* out of my mind.

Paris, 1879

13

The Livery Stable

That winter was the harshest anyone could remember. It began long before the start of the new year, with slashing rain that turned to stinging sleet and scoured our faces. For weeks, thick gray clouds muffled the sun, and a frigid wind knifed around window frames. Ice glazed the bricks and cobblestones, so that walking was nearly impossible on the steep streets that climbed through Montmartre. Blankets of snow smothered the rooftops, heaped puffy crowns on the chimney pots—and transformed even our drab neighborhood into a scene as magical as any on the stage of the Opéra. But then soot tarnished the snow, turning it as dreary as the skies, and the magic disappeared. My hands and face grew chapped and rough, my eyes streamed with tears, and my nose dripped. The cold settled into our bones and stayed.

One blustery Sunday afternoon, when walking failed to warm us and we had no money to spend at a café, Jean-Pierre suggested that we take shelter in his quarters at the livery. Head bent against the driving snow, I followed him blindly through a maze of narrow streets near the train tracks leading from Gare Saint-Lazare, and arrived at the stable breathless and laughing.

Once my eyes had grown used to the dim light, Jean-Pierre led me from stall to stall and introduced me to each horse as though it were an old friend. Proudly Jean-Pierre showed off the gleaming calèches and landaus and other fine carriages that he helped to keep clean and polished. Then I clambered up a flimsy ladder after him to a loft under the roof. One corner was furnished with a leather-bound trunk and a straw pallet covered with a rough blanket.

"Welcome to my home," he said, offering me a hand up. "In exchange for a place to sleep, I'm also the night watchman."

"You live here?" I asked.

"*Mais oui,*" he said. "It was supposed to be temporary, but I've come to like it well enough."

The loft smelled strongly of hay and manure, but it also felt snug. Seeing how I shivered, Jean-Pierre took the blanket from his pallet and draped it around my shoulders. He found a couple of withered apples in his trunk, cut them into quarters, and offered them to me. Below us, his fellow residents snorted and stomped and banged the wooden sides of their stalls.

"But where is your family?" I asked, breathing in the sharp sweetness of the apple. I vaguely remembered his round, jolly mother and tall, silent father.

"After my grandfather died last year, my parents took the little ones to live with my grandmother on the farm near Rouen. I decided to stay in Paris. I prefer the city, but I do miss them—at times very much."

I nodded sympathetically. "I wouldn't want to be away from my sisters—especially Charlotte. And even Antoinette, maddening as she can be. She's the practical one in our family. I can't imagine doing without them." An image of my father's pale, gaunt face flitted through my memory.

"And your mother?" he asked, biting into an apple. "You often speak of your sisters, but you hardly mention your mother."

I grimaced. "She's my mother," I said. "But she drinks."

"Maybe she drinks to forget her hardships."

"*Oui*, but she forgets about *us!*" Was it disloyal to tell him this? Perhaps, but it was also the painful truth. "A glass of absinthe means more to her than feeding her daughters. How can she *do* that?" I cried.

"Perhaps she can't help herself. Try to forgive her."

"It's hard to forgive her when Charlotte is weak with hunger," I said.

Jean-Pierre reached for my hand and held it for a moment before he let go, and we fell again to eating apples. "Take mine, too," he said, pushing two apple quarters toward me. "For Charlotte."

AFTER A LONG ABSENCE, Tante Hélène finally came to visit us that winter. Worried that we might not have warm clothes, which of course we did not, she brought us a heavy military coat that had once belonged to her son who had been badly wounded years earlier in the war between France and Prussia. She didn't mention Antoinette's green silk dress or the harsh words that had passed between us, and neither did I.

The coat was much too big for any of us, but we took turns wearing it. I missed my old tartan shawl; the gray one that Antoinette had given me to replace it was pretty but not nearly as warm.

My sisters and I were glad to spend most of our time at the Palais Garnier, where ceramic stoves produced some heat in the practice rooms, even though it was never enough. It was hard for us to dance when we were shivering with cold. When we weren't doing our exercises, we huddled around the stoves, sharing coats and whatever else we could find to keep ourselves warm. At home we often simply stayed in bed.

On one of the coldest days of January—it was Charlotte's turn to wear the old army coat, and I could not stop my teeth from chattering—I found Jean-Pierre outside the Palais Garnier, waiting to walk home with me, as he often did when the Cassatts had chosen not to leave their warm apartment. When he noticed that my hands were nearly purple with cold, he took off his gloves and gave them to me. I protested that I couldn't take them—surely he needed them!—but he brushed aside my arguments.

"I have another pair," he said, smoothing the soft black leather over my fingers. I hoped he was telling the truth, even though I doubted that his other gloves were nearly so fine as these.

ONE BY ONE, we began to fall ill. The headache and fever began during a performance; my legs felt weak, and twice I stumbled. The next day I coughed and thrashed in our bed, my head pounding, my body shaking with chills. Every bone ached, every muscle throbbed. There would be fines for my absence, I knew— we were expected to be present no matter how terrible we felt—but I was too sick to leave the bed.

On the fourth day spots appeared on my chest and stomach and quickly spread to every part of my body. It was February 17, my fifteenth birthday, and I lay there in feverish misery. Sometimes I dreamed that I was with Jean-Pierre, eating apples.

Soon Charlotte complained of the same symptoms.

At first Antoinette remained healthy. She shuddered and kept her distance from us, saying she didn't want to catch whatever we had. "What good will it do for me to stay here? Misery loves company, I know, but it would be much better for me to keep away."

Within days she, too, became ill.

Maman had no notion of what to do for us. Finally she said, "I'm sending for Hélène." It was the first time I'd ever heard her admit to needing our aunt's help.

When Tante Hélène arrived, she looked us over carefully, saw the spots on our chests, and announced her diagnosis: typhus. "From lice and fleas," she explained.

She made broth and spoon-fed it to us, one at a time. She mixed ground mustard and flour with water and spread the paste on layers of newspaper to make a poultice, which she laid on our chests to draw out the fever. When we cried that we were being burned, she rubbed our reddened skin with goose fat. She brewed a syrup of onion juice and sugar to treat our hacking coughs. She insisted that the straw in our mattress be burned and our bedding washed in hot water, and she lectured Maman sternly that a laundress, of all people, should be able to keep her daughters in clean linens. Maman silently accepted the criticism, her head bowed. She hadn't known, she murmured; she had no idea.

We, her daughters, looked at one another. Maman was rarely sober these days. She would go down to the street to buy bread, and somehow get no farther than the shop that sold spirits. Tante Hélène left our mother with detailed instructions for our care and a severe warning to avoid drink, but we understood that we would have to take care of one another.

For many days we felt too weak to leave our two rooms. I thought constantly of Jean-Pierre, alone in his loft above the stables, and I worried. If he was ill, who would take care of him? Who would even know?

As it turned out, he was quite well, but he'd been working long hours to take over the duties of several grooms and coachmen who were ill; two had died. We were recovering when he came to the door one day with a jar of fruit preserves given him by Mademoiselle Mary Cassatt. "It's said to help restore your strength," he said, handing me the jar.

"How did you know we were ill?" I asked hoarsely.

"Your friend the tobacconist," he explained. "I stopped in at his shop to inquire about you. He mentioned that his wife is doing very poorly."

"But we're getting better now," Charlotte volunteered. "Maybe you should take the preserves down to Madame Lerat."

"What a lovely thought," I said, already sorry to be giving up such a nice treat.

"Don't be ridiculous," Antoinette objected, her voice little better than a croak. "We need it ourselves if we're ever to get back to dancing."

For two days we discussed the preserves, and in the end Antoinette and I ate it, under Charlotte's withering stare.

WHEN ANTOINETTE and I were finally able to drag ourselves back to the Opéra, we learned that so many dancers had fallen ill with typhus that several performances had had to be canceled. I was unwilling to lose any more of my meager pay, but the main reason Antoinette was eager to return so soon was that she was bent on resuming her visits to the *foyer de la danse*. Monsieur Chevreul had vanished suddenly from her life, having switched his interest and his patronage to a *premier sujet,* a dancer in a higher level of the *corps de ballet*.

"I'll never forgive him," Antoinette declared. "Never! The man hasn't the slightest idea of the meaning of loyalty."

Meanwhile, she'd had no luck in finding a new "friend."

OUR STRENGTH slowly continued to return, and with it came the first faint signs of spring. When the Cassatt family didn't require the services of their coachman, Jean-Pierre waited outside the Palais Garnier to accompany me home after performances, and we resumed our Sunday walks.

On one such walk along Boulevard de Clichy, near Place Pigalle, Jean-Pierre pointed out Mademoiselle Cassatt's studio, above a pastry shop. "Second floor, the two middle windows. Sometimes I'm asked to drive Mademoiselle Lydia to the studio, or to take her home again, although it's only a few blocks. She's not well, you know. Mademoiselle Mary always walks to her studio. Now that the weather is warmer, I drive her to the Bois de Boulogne nearly every morning, to ride her horse."

"I'd love to go there again," I said wistfully.

He grinned. "Better take swimming lessons."

"Without the boat ride!" I replied.

14

Notre-Dame de Lorette

Charlotte woke me early on a Sunday in April. "Marie!" she whispered urgently. "Get up! It's time."

It was barely daylight, and my body craved sleep. Antoinette had tumbled into bed beside us only two or three hours earlier. "What? What is it?" I murmured.

"It's Easter. You said we'd go to Mass today. Don't you remember? We even went to confession. You promised, Marie!"

"Did I?" I hadn't really forgotten, but I had injured my foot the previous night, landing awkwardly from a jump in the last act. It throbbed painfully. I looked at Charlotte's pleading eyes and relented. "All right. Give me a little time."

I pulled on my often-mended chemise and patched skirt, but the drawstring in the skirt broke and had to be knotted and rethreaded. I threw a shawl around my shoulders and shuffled into my sabots. Antoinette burrowed deeper into her pillow. Maman's deep snores rattled in her throat. Charlotte didn't bother to try to rouse them—it would have been hopeless—and we crept out of our dingy rooms, shutting the door softly. We were already late.

The church of Notre-Dame de Lorette was a half dozen streets away on Rue Laffitte, at the lower end of Rue des Martyrs. At the time of my father's death, Maman had managed to scrape together a few coins to pay the priest for a funeral Mass, but Papa had ended up buried among the poor in a potter's field. Since then we had attended Mass only occasionally. Days earlier I had given in to Charlotte's pleas, promising her we'd go to Easter Mass and waiting in a long line to make my confession to the priest: *Bless me, Father, for I have sinned* . . . Most of my sins involved telling lies.

The neighborhood surrounding the church was home to many women of bad reputation, from ordinary prostitutes to courtesans kept in fine style by their wealthy lovers. Many of these fallen women attended Mass at Notre-Dame de Lorette; they were known in the neighborhood as *lorettes*. We could have gone to another church—there were several close by—but we felt that Lorette was ours.

Whenever I entered this church, a sense of awe swept over me—inspired not just by the grandeur of the building but by the sense of mystery I felt there. I dipped my fingers in the holy water, making the sign of the cross on my breast, and breathed in the heady scent of incense.

The church was filled. Closest to the altar, gentlemen in morning coats knelt on velvet cushions next to ladies in modest dresses with sweeping skirts, pelisses trimmed with fur, and bonnets framed with lace. Among these well-dressed worshippers, I was certain, were at least a few of the gentlemen who regularly visited the *foyer de la danse,* now kneeling piously beside their wives. Their prayer books lay open but their eyes were fastened on a row of fashionably dressed women with no husbands at their elbows: the *lorettes.*

Charlotte and I crowded in among the poor at the rear of the church and knelt on the cold stone floor. While the priest droned on about sin and repentance, I gazed up at the gilded ceiling, the paintings in the dome above the altar, the rows of thick marble columns. Candles flickered in the shadows. Motes of dust danced in the watery light that fell in thin streams from the high windows. Bells rang. The priest in his gold-trimmed vestments raised the jeweled silver chalice and chanted the words of the Mass in a language we didn't know but felt we somehow understood.

The ladies in rustling silk and the gentlemen with flowers in their buttonholes stepped forward to receive the sacrament. They were followed by the *lorettes,* heads bowed, forgiven now of all their sins, on the great feast of Easter.

Finally it was our turn, the poor in our ragged clothes, our empty stomachs and hungry hearts waiting to be filled.

CHARLOTTE and I decided to take the long way home in order to admire the Easter finery of people flocking the streets and climbing into waiting carriages. We walked slowly, I favoring my injured foot, along Rue de Châteaudun and then out Boulevard de Clichy. I glanced up at Mademoiselle Cassatt's studio and paused to peer into the window of the pastry shop on the ground floor to study the posters displayed there. Vivid red letters on a green background caught my attention—I made out something about ART and ARTISTS. Slowly I read the words aloud: AN EXHIBITION OF PAINTINGS BY A GROUP OF INDEPENDENT ARTISTS. I easily—and proudly—recognized Edgar Degas and Mary Cassatt on the list of names. The opening date was April 10, three days past.

"Is your statue in the exhibition, Marie?" Charlotte asked.

"I have no idea. Maybe it's there. Maybe he's forgotten about it. I see Monsieur Degas at the Opéra, but he doesn't speak to me, doesn't even seem to recognize me, and he hasn't called for me to pose for him again. Maybe he won't finish it. I wish I knew."

The thought that the sculpture might never be completed saddened me. It was as though some part of myself would be left unfinished.

———

EVEN NOW, it hurts to think about Antoinette. Her flirtations in the *foyer de la danse* were no longer lighthearted amusements but had become serious endeavors. Ever since Monsieur Chevreul shifted his attentions to another dancer, my sister was more determined than ever to find a wealthy man who would make her his mistress and provide for her.

"Look, Marie," she would say, "once I find a man who's both able and willing to give me what I deserve, I'll set something aside for you and Charlotte. But you must not tell Maman. You know that anything we give her goes to the absinthe seller."

At times I envied Antoinette. When she mentioned that Monsieur Degas had summoned her to pose for him again, I nearly wept with jealousy. Had he changed his mind and decided to use Antoinette, instead, for his sculpture? I would not forgive him if he did. Nor would I forgive my sister!

I tearfully demanded to know exactly how he had her pose.

"*Mon Dieu*, Marie, what's got into you?" she cried. "It's just another one of his dance pictures—actually an old one that he began a couple of years ago. And posing for him is no joy, I promise you! I have to hold an *arabesque* on *pointe* until I think I'll drop."

I didn't believe her easy answer, but I said nothing.

She raced on, "I don't know how you put up with him. Degas must be the oddest man I've ever met. He isn't married, and as far as I can tell, he doesn't even have a mistress. Not like the other artists! Oh, I know a thing or two about some of his friends. I see them in the cabarets, and I've heard the gossip that they sleep with their models and have children by them—and then, after two or three brats are born, perhaps they marry the mother, or perhaps not! So why doesn't your Monsieur Degas do that, eh? Because he's peculiar, that's why!"

"He's not *my* Monsieur Degas," I protested. "He's an artist, and I think his art is all that really matters to him."

"Well, then, what about Mademoiselle Cassatt? You've met her, haven't you?"

"*Oui,* I have."

"Don't you think they're lovers?"

"In the beginning I thought so," I admitted, "but later I changed my mind. Now I think they're just friends. She's an artist, too."

"You honestly believe that a man and woman can just be friends?" Antoinette jeered. "Oh, you really are naive, Marie!"

"Not naive," I said, "but not like you. And yes, I do believe they can."

For a moment my thoughts darted to Jean-Pierre and then skittered away. Something had begun to change between us, and I didn't want to think about that yet—or mention it to Antoinette.

THE NEXT TIME Antoinette went to Monsieur Degas's studio, she brought me back a souvenir: a sheet of tracing paper folded into a square. When I opened the paper—the kind he used to work from one image to another, reversing a figure or making some other change—I saw that it was one of the early sketches he had made of me. Just a few delicate lines, but it clearly was *me*.

Antoinette grinned impishly. "So he finally convinced you to pose in the nude."

"He pays more for it," I said, and immediately wished I hadn't told her. I didn't want her to ask me *how much* more. "Why did he give you this drawing?"

She hooted with laughter. "Oh, you are a goose! I *took* it, Marie!"

"You stole it?" I was incredulous. *"You stole it?"* I repeated, remembering that I had once considered doing exactly that.

"There were lots of them spread out all over his worktable, and it was the easiest thing in the world just to pick up one little drawing." She shrugged. "He'll never miss it. He's got dozens more."

I refolded the paper with care. "And the sculpture? Did you see it? Or a little figure made of wire?"

"No, but I did see a kind of metal framework with blobs of wax stuck on it. I knew it was you from the sketches."

So he *was* working on it, then! He hadn't stopped after all! Or at least he hadn't abandoned it completely.

Later, when I was alone, I unfolded the drawing and studied it closely. He had made it from the side: I stood in profile, head up, hands behind my back. I loved it, but I hated the idea that Antoinette had taken it. I was pulled first one way, then the other: If I took the drawing back to Monsieur Degas, he would know it had been stolen and maybe blame me for it. If I didn't, it was possible that he'd never miss it. As Antoinette said, he'd made dozens of sketches—surely this one wouldn't matter. Back and forth I went: *on the one hand . . . on the other . . .*

Finally I decided that when he summoned me to pose for him again I would take it to him, explaining that it was a mistake. Until he sent for me, I would keep the drawing on the bottom of my wooden trunk, laid flat to press out the creases.

But Monsieur Degas didn't send for me, and I kept the drawing. Now I would have to add *theft* to my list of sins.

15

Tea with the Artist

Somehow I could not forget about Mademoiselle Cassatt. I went out of my way to walk up Boulevard de Clichy, just so I could pass by the building where she had her studio. I would stand for long minutes gazing at the elegant pastries displayed in the window of la Couronne d'Or, and I did this so often that the owner of the patisserie began to nod and wave, and once even came out to give me a bit of stale rum cake.

Then one day, after I had delivered a basket of clean linens to one of Maman's customers, I climbed boldly up two flights of stairs to a door I thought must be Mademoiselle Cassatt's. I listened: I could hear nothing inside. Maybe she wasn't even there. Gathering my courage, I knocked.

A dog began barking madly—Batty, of course—and a woman's voice called out, "*Oui? Qui est là?* Who's there?"

I turned, ready to run down the stairs, when the door opened a crack and Mademoiselle Cassatt peered out, struggling to keep the yapping dog from getting past her skirts. "Marie? Is it you?"

I stammered an apology, too witless to think of a possible excuse for being at her door. But she snatched up the dog, smiling, and opened the door wide. "Come in, then."

Leaving my sabots by the door, as we did at home, I stepped inside. The lovely, sunlit room was more like a lady's parlor than a place of work, although an easel stood in one corner, with tubes of paint and jars of brushes lined up in neat rows beside it. A carpet, patterned with red and blue swirls, covered part of the gleaming wood floor. Near a pair of tall windows facing the street—the windows Jean-Pierre had pointed out—a planter holding bunches of hyacinths stood next to an armchair that was covered in black-and-purple-striped satin. A low table was set with a delicate white teacup and saucer, rimmed in gold. On the mantel above the fireplace, a clock chimed the quarter hour.

"Not quite like Monsieur Degas's atelier, is it?" she said with a laugh, guessing my thoughts. "Now," asked Mademoiselle Cassatt, "what brings you here, Marie? Did Monsieur Degas send you?"

"I've come to say hello to Batty," I said, as the little dog sniffed my ankles. It was the first thing that came into my head.

My explanation must have seemed absurd, but Mademoiselle Cassatt merely smiled. "You've met Batty before?"

"*Oui*, Mademoiselle. I once brought him to your home after he had visited Monsieur Degas."

"*Bien sûr.* I'd forgotten. *Alors*, now that you're here, may I offer you a cup of tea? I was about to have one myself."

I quickly accepted the invitation and, to cover my embarrassment, picked up the excitable Batty, who immediately calmed down.

"You may look around, if you like. The water is just coming to a boil."

Carrying Batty, who nuzzled my ear, I stepped over to the easel. It held a painting of Mademoiselle Lydia, dressed in the loveliest pink bonnet and dress, trimmed in white, and in long white gloves. She sat in the striped chair, holding the gold-rimmed cup and saucer. Behind her the hyacinths added little dashes of purple and white.

"Oh," I said, letting out a long breath. "It's so beautiful."

"It's not quite finished," said Mademoiselle Cassatt, pouring water into a Japanese pot with a bamboo handle. "My sister hasn't been feeling well. She's my favorite model; no one can hold a pose as well as she can, but it's hard on her. It takes so much of her strength." She gave me a quick, sad smile and set a second cup and saucer on the table. "As I recall, you have two sisters, do you not? Both dancers, like you?"

"*Oui*, Mademoiselle. Antoinette and Charlotte." I was surprised that she remembered, for I'd mentioned my sisters in a conversation that took place more than a year before, on my first visit to Monsieur Degas's studio.

Mademoiselle Cassatt removed the artist's smock that covered her plain blue dress, poured tea into the two gold-rimmed cups, and arranged a little bowl of sugar and a pitcher of cream beside them. "Sit down, Marie," she said, gesturing toward the striped armchair and drawing up a rush-covered stool for herself.

I perched uneasily on the edge of the chair, dreadfully aware of my poor clothes. I had never been served tea like this, nor had I ever drunk from anything so delicate, and I was immensely afraid of spilling the tea or breaking the cup. I put Batty down on the floor and watched Mademoiselle Cassatt to see what I must do next. I was both ashamed that I had come here so boldly and thrilled by the opportunity to be taking tea with such a fine lady.

"I'm sorry I have nothing to offer you to eat," she said, adding a half spoonful of sugar to her tea; I did the same. "The patisserie downstairs offers constant temptation, which I do my best to resist. Now tell me, Marie, have you been posing for Monsieur Degas?" She poured a little cream into her cup and stirred gently; I copied her.

"*Non,* Mademoiselle. Not for a very long time. He said he'd call for me when he needed me to finish the statuette. I wonder if you could tell me—is it in the exhibition? I saw the poster in the window downstairs."

"It's not, but one never knows about Monsieur Degas."

Batty trotted over to sit by his mistress, who scratched his rough, wiry coat and gazed at him fondly. "I've just had an idea, Marie. My father and I are making a long journey to Italy this summer. My mother and Lydia will remain in Paris. Batty gets very lonely and out of sorts without me— don't you, Batty?—and neither my mother nor my sister is interested in taking him for romps in the park. Usually I engage the porter to do this for me when I'm away, but I'm wondering—would you consider assuming this responsibility? Coming by for him three or four times a week and taking him to Place d'Anvers? We'll be gone at least three months. I'd pay you for your trouble, of course."

Like to? I was delighted—so delighted that I sloshed tea into the saucer. "Ah, *oui,* Mademoiselle, of course! You may depend on me."

"*Très bien!* We're leaving about the first of June. Come by to see me again in a few weeks, and we'll work out the particulars. Perhaps by then we'll have news of Monsieur Degas's progress with your statuette."

I managed to finish my tea without mishap, thanked her as well as I knew how, and rushed home with my good news, trying to remember every detail to tell Antoinette and

Charlotte—and later, Jean-Pierre—about having tea with Mademoiselle Cassatt.

IF THE WINTER of 1879 was especially harsh, the summer made up for it. That was the summer I realized I had fallen in love.

After Mademoiselle Cassatt and her father left for Italy, her mother and sister remained in Paris, requiring Jean-Pierre to drive them to milliners' shops and dressmakers' salons, to dinners with friends, to picnics in the Bois de Boulogne. Jean-Pierre was supposed to have a day off on Sunday or Monday, but whenever the Cassatt ladies wanted to be taken somewhere, the coachman had to be ready. And I had promised to pick up Batty four times a week at 13 Avenue Trudaine and take him to Place d'Anvers to chase a red rubber ball. Madame Cassatt or Mademoiselle Lydia or the haughty maid handed me fifty centimes each time—two francs a week—for which I was grateful.

There was never enough time left over for Jean-Pierre and me to make another trip by omnibus to the Bois, and so our entertainment continued to be long, rambling walks. Sometimes we strolled along the river Seine or lingered in the formal gardens of the Tuileries near the Louvre, eating fruit ices and licking the sticky syrup from our fingers. Most often, though, we climbed the cobbled streets of Montmartre, past artists' studios and bustling cafés and the Moulin de la Galette, until we reached the highest point of the butte.

We wandered through vineyards and wheat fields, and among old windmills where the wheat was ground, the sails creaking as they turned in the breeze.

I remember what I was wearing on one particular July afternoon—a dark blue linen skirt woven with a narrow brown stripe, and a chemise of pale blue muslin gathered low on my neck with a ribbon. I remember that we stopped along the way to buy bread and cheese and a jug of cider. It was just Jean-Pierre and me that day—I've forgotten why Charlotte hadn't come with us, as she often did—and suddenly I felt shy and self-conscious. I suspect that he felt the same. But it was so peaceful there, beyond the clamor of the city, that our shyness began to melt away.

We lounged in the sweet-smelling grass, eating the bread and cheese, saying little. The warm sun slid over our skin. Wisps of music floated up from the dance hall below us. Jean-Pierre picked a bunch of grapes from a gnarled vine and bent over me, holding a fat purple grape gently between his teeth. He came closer, lowering his face until the grape barely touched my lips, and I opened my mouth and took it from him. One by one he fed me the grapes, his lips grazing mine.

"Your turn," he said, rolling onto his back and handing me the half-eaten bunch of grapes.

Soon the grapes were no longer important, and Jean-Pierre pulled me close in a passionate kiss.

The embarrassment of this struck us both at once. We leaped to our feet and began to chatter about the need to leave: It had to be getting late; the horses at the stable had to be fed and watered; I'd best find out where Charlotte had got to; it was time to take Batty to Place d'Anvers. We plunged down the steep steps and crooked streets of Montmartre and parted as though nothing unusual had happened. But we both knew it had, and I cherished the memory of that blissful afternoon long after the days and nights had again turned cold and bitter.

16

The Coryphée

In September the *petits rats* and members of the *corps de ballet* were once more required to undergo dance examinations. All three of us had passed the spring examinations, although none of us had advanced to the next level. But the autumn examinations were different: I not only passed but I won a promotion to *coryphée*. Charlotte earned praise from the judges and a hint that within two years, three at most, she would be in the *quadrille*. And this time Antoinette was made a *petit sujet*! We all had reason to celebrate.

"Now, *ma petite* Marie," said Antoinette, "you have no more excuses not to attend the *foyer de la danse* with me. If only you could put on a bit of weight, you'd have no trouble at all attracting the attention of a generous *abonné*. Most men prefer girls who are a bit plump—not skinny little sticks like you!"

"Then since, as you say, I'm a 'skinny little stick,' there's no need for me to visit the *foyer*," I retorted.

But Maman had other ideas. "Marie, I beg you," she began, "listen to me."

My mother's hands were rough and peeling, her arms scarred with burns from the flatirons. Her hair, once thick and gleaming and the color of honey, hung limp and faded. Her face was blotchy. Her teeth had loosened, and there were dark gaps where two were missing. Her eyes were worst of all: Bloodshot and watery, they seemed empty and hopeless. Maman was perhaps thirty-five, about the same age as Mademoiselle Mary Cassatt, but she looked like an old woman, used up and exhausted.

"Do you think you're too good to do whatever must be done so that we can eat and clothe ourselves?" my mother demanded, in a voice as harsh as metal scraping metal. "Look at us, in rags—except for what Antoinette is given by her gentleman friends. Are you such a fine lady, Marie, that you're above accepting the favors of these gentlemen and doing for them whatever they may ask of you in return?"

I stared at my mother, my stomach churning. "Maman, are you suggesting that I become a—"

"*Mais non*, Marie. But you earn next to nothing as a dancer! All I'm asking is that you make yourself available for the friendship of men who may offer it." Then she added, "Remember, you're no better than the rest of us."

"I'm better than you want me to be," I said. "I don't need beautiful clothes or jewels. All I want is to dance."

"Pretty words indeed," said my mother. "But you think only of yourself—of what *you* want. We must eat. We must put clothes on our backs and a roof over our heads."

"If you drank less, our money would go farther!" I said, the words bursting out before I could stop them. She stared at me with wounded eyes, saying nothing. I regretted my disrespect, although I knew I was right.

But was she also right? Was I really only being selfish in my refusal to go to the *foyer de la danse?* Maybe that was a sacrifice I had to make, the price I had to pay, in order to dance. And I still felt that I owed a debt to Tante Hélène.

The next week, when Antoinette hurried to the *foyer de la danse* between the acts of *Coppélia,* I was with her.

I LOVED TO DANCE *Coppélia,* not only because I liked the music but also because I enjoyed the story—about a clever young girl named Swanilda and her sweetheart, Franz; a toy maker called Dr. Coppélius, who dreams of making a doll that will come to life; and, of course, the beautiful mechanical doll, Coppélia. The mayor of Swanilda's village announces a celebration in honor of the town's new bells and promises a bag of gold to every couple who marry on that day. I'd been assigned the role of one of the bridegrooms, so

I was costumed not in a gauzy tutu and *pointe* shoes but in tight-fitting trousers and jacket, my thick braid stuffed under a cap. I had even painted black mustaches on my upper lip. It was in this masculine dress that I marched into the *foyer de la danse*.

Antoinette, one of the village brides, frowned her disapproval. "The other girls have better sense than to come here in male costume," she informed me.

"You said I should come," I insisted stubbornly. "And so here I am."

"At least take off that ridiculous cap," she said. "And let me wipe off the mustaches. I'll paint them on again for you before the next act."

Antoinette's lips were set in a tight line as she erased my mustaches with a handkerchief. That done, she assumed the role of hostess and began introducing me to the gentlemen of the *foyer de la danse*. "This is my sister, Marie, who has just been made a *coryphée*! Just look at her—isn't she the most enchanting little thing? 'Exquisite,' I've heard people say. And, of course, she's even more adorable when she's not dressed up like a boy. Be sure to watch for her in the next act! Madame Théodore has been raving about her for some time now. Even Monsieur Perrot has taken notice of her talents. Wait and see, she'll be *une étoile* one of these days—a star!"

On and on she prattled, while I stood by awkwardly, unable to think of a single clever word to say. Antoinette was a mistress of the art of sprightly banter, and the gentlemen did their part, attempting to engage me in conversation, but I was struck dumb.

"Tell me, my dear," said a red-faced gentleman, peering at me through his pince-nez, "what sort of amusements do you prefer?"

I stared at him, my mouth dry as sand, my mind blank as stone.

"Perhaps our young dancer is clever at cards," suggested his friend, a skewer-thin man with foul breath. "She might possibly enjoy a game of bezique?"

I shifted uncomfortably, saw the frozen smile on Antoinette's lips, and knew that if I didn't say something quickly, she'd supply an answer for me.

"I read," I blurted out.

Antoinette rolled her eyes and the men gaped, as if I had just announced that I swallowed flaming swords. Then they burst into loud guffaws. "Read!" they chortled.

"Our little gamine claims that she likes to read!" bellowed the red-faced man, his pince-nez dropping from his nose. They laughed so heartily that they had to dab their eyes with their monogrammed linen handkerchiefs before they could speak again. "Now tell us, *ma chère* Marie, what do you 'read'? The novels of Victor Hugo? Émile Zola? Or do you prefer the classics—Molière, perhaps?"

I didn't know what they were talking about, but I understood that they were mocking me. "I read the newspaper, Messieurs," I said, trying to muster a smile. *"Le Figaro."*

This was not a lie, or even much of an exaggeration. Over the past year, with Charlotte's help, I had become a slow but careful reader—although I still couldn't write any more than my own name and the names of my family members.

I was much relieved when the callboy summoned the dancers to take their places onstage for the wedding scene, and the bell rang signaling the audience to return to their seats for the next act. The *abonnés* bent low over my hand and kissed it, still snickering, "She reads! Our little dancer reads!" They hastened off to share this great joke with their friends.

Antoinette didn't try to hide her disgust. "What on earth possessed you to say such a thing?" she demanded, hastily repainting my mustaches. "You've certainly ruined your chances, telling that stupid little tale!"

"So much the better," I said defiantly. "Then I have no need to visit the *foyer de la danse* again."

I WAS DANCING better than ever. The years of training, of daily practice at the *barre,* of sore muscles and aching feet— they all seemed to be yielding their reward. For a long time I had wondered what kind of dancer I might become. Antoinette's dream had always been to dance the romantic adagio roles. In many ways she was naturally gifted for such parts. Her extension—the height to which she could raise her working leg in *développé*—was splendid, like the unfolding of a butterfly's wing. And she could hold the most difficult positions longer than most dancers, even the more experienced *sujets*. Her *port de bras*—the way she held her arms—was graceful, the line from her fingertip to the arch of her foot elegant. Her dancing showed grace and tenderness, and if she had been willing to work a little harder there was no doubt that great success was within her reach. I had none of those qualities, and no matter how I drove myself, I knew I would never have them.

Charlotte, now nine, had begun learning to dance on *pointe*. Her talent was obvious. She was light and quick—very quick—and her turns were fast and accurate. *In a few years,* I thought, *Charlotte might have a chance at the allegro roles.*

I was not as elegant as Antoinette or as nimble as Charlotte, but I was very strong. My jumps were high and my landings solid, with no wobble. Madame Théodore had encouraging words for me: "You have legs like springs," she said. "I almost believe you could fly, if I asked you to. Work very hard and someday you could do well in travesty roles."

These were men's roles taken by female dancers. Because there were almost no male dancers in the Paris Opéra ballet, the roles of the prince in *Giselle* and of Franz, Dr. Coppélius, the mayor, and—of course—the bridegrooms in *Coppélia* were always performed by ballerinas in male costumes. Naturally, Madame Théodore's encouragement pleased me. Believing now that I had a real future at the Opéra, I pushed myself harder than ever to prove myself.

Although pleased with my progress, Maman was not satisfied, for I continued to avoid the *foyer de la danse*. "It might be years before you get your first solo role," she said. "And how are we to live in the meantime? I do all that I can, but my wages don't begin to stretch far enough, even with what Antoinette gives me. I have no talent like yours—what do I know besides the washtub and the flatiron? Nothing! But you are young and talented! You must find a suitable patron, a gentleman who will take care of you. Antoinette understands this—why don't you? Even if you don't want to do it for yourself, Marie, then do it for Charlotte. She's not old enough to look after herself. Every franc that you bring home, every *sou*, will help."

I did understand—our circumstances were not unusual. Most of my friends were expected to help support their families. But still I resisted the *foyer de la danse*—and not only because I didn't enjoy the flirtation or because I found the *abonnés* appallingly dull. And my resistance was certainly not because I didn't know how terribly poor we were or because I had forgotten the debt I believed I still owed Tante Hélène for the dress.

I resisted because I was in love with Jean-Pierre.

I tried to keep my feelings a secret. I didn't want Antoinette to know that I had a sweetheart, because I knew what she'd tell me: "You'd be mad to consider taking such a lover! What can a mere stable hand do for you?" I didn't want Maman to know, either—she had eloped with a poor tailor and paid a price for it. But, of course, Charlotte suspected how I felt.

She adored Jean-Pierre, and he was always kind to her. "My own sister is about her age," he told me. In the beginning Charlotte had gone everywhere with us, and she continued to expect to go everywhere with us, until I explained that Jean-Pierre and I were sweethearts and that at times we wished to be alone.

"Oh, I've known that all along," she said airily. "But don't worry—I won't tell Antoinette. Or Maman."

I SAW MADEMOISELLE CASSATT only briefly, on the last day of September, after she had returned from Italy. She paid me my two francs for the week and thanked me. My services as Batty's playmate were no longer needed. "Perhaps another time," she said with her warm smile, adding a bonus of another franc.

I was sad to have my little job come to an end, sad not to have Batty's company, but sadder yet that I could not think of an excuse to visit Mademoiselle Cassatt's studio and to spend another hour in her beautiful, orderly world.

Paris, 1880

17

Lucien Daudet

My sixteenth birthday fell on a Tuesday, and as it happened, that was the day Monsieur Degas summoned me to pose again for the statuette. "In your practice clothes," he said.

I wondered why he wanted me to wear a tutu after all the times I had posed for him without clothes. Naturally, I didn't ask.

Mademoiselle Cassatt was in his studio when I arrived. She looked exhausted. The studio was littered with black-and-white pictures they had made on the printing press.

"Oh, Marie, I'm glad you've come," said Mademoiselle Cassatt. "I'm so tired I can hardly speak my own name." Pushing a pile of prints to one side, she sank onto the divan and rubbed her eyes. "We're getting ready for the spring exhibition and preparing a new journal to be published at the same time. Edgar, Marie's statuette will be ready as well, will it not?"

"*Oui, oui,* it will. Certainly," he growled.

Then I saw it: the wax figure on a low table. The statuette was about the size of Charlotte and looked even more like me than the wire sketch had.

I took my place on the model's stand and submitted to Monsieur Degas's scrutiny. "She's grown a little taller, a little more muscular since I made my first sketches," he said, speaking over his shoulder to Mademoiselle Cassatt. "But the qualities that appealed to me then haven't changed. She's still a gamine, with the look of an impudent child of the streets. One sees it clearly in her expression—alert, wary, sometimes sly. A bit rude, perhaps, when it's necessary." He spoke to me. "Do you agree with that, *ma petite?*"

"*Oui,*" I murmured, as he expected. I *didn't* agree, but it would have been impudent to say so!

He spoke again to Mademoiselle Cassatt. "Did I tell you, Mary, that I've employed one of the seamstresses at the Opéra to make a dance costume—tutu, tights, bodice, even little slippers. 'It must be quite small,' I instructed her. 'To fit a small, thin child.' She promised to have it ready soon."

"That's nice," said Mademoiselle Cassatt drowsily.

Ordered a dance costume? For the statuette? But why? I wondered. He stepped close and tipped my chin up slightly.

"I've visited a glazier's shop and ordered a vitrine," he con-

tinued, "a cabinet to be made to my specifications, somewhat
more than a meter high, of beveled glass with brass fittings.
Also a wigmaker—did I tell you that? But I've not been
happy with those negotiations. The wigmaker wants to use
horsehair, and I've insisted that only real human hair will do."

"Ummmm," murmured Mademoiselle Cassatt.

I couldn't imagine what he was thinking, but it was not
my place to ask questions.

"That will be all for today, Mademoiselle," he said, after
only an hour or so. He gave me two francs along with a pat
on the shoulder. "It's nearly finished, but I'll need you once
or twice more for the final touches to the face. Agreed?"

Mademoiselle Cassatt had fallen asleep on the divan.
"She's been working hard," Monsieur Degas said, regarding
her. "She came back from Italy exhausted from her travels,
and now she's determined to produce two major paintings a
month for the spring exhibition. But she's here every day,
working with me on the etchings we've planned for the journal. Quite a lot for anyone."

"*Oui*, Monsieur." I had already reached the door when I
stopped and turned back. "What are you calling the statuette, Monsieur? Have you given it a name?"

"*Petite danseuse de quatorze ans,*" he said. *Little Dancer
Aged Fourteen.*

ON THE WAY HOME I stopped at the tobacconist's shop, asked
Monsieur Lerat for the tin he kept under the counter, and

dropped in one of the two francs Monsieur Degas had paid me. The other I would give to Maman.

Usually Monsieur Lerat teased me. "You'll be a rich woman someday, Marie." But that day there was no light-hearted teasing. "Is something wrong?" I asked.

"Madame Lerat," he said sadly. "She's very ill, and the doctors have no hope for her. Consumption," he added, placing his hand on his chest.

"I'm sorry," I said.

Scarcely a week later Charlotte and I saw two men carrying a body wrapped in a white sheet out of the Lerats' rooms at the rear of the shop. Monsieur Lerat walked behind the body, clutching the hands of two young boys, his shaggy head bent. We made the sign of the cross as they passed by.

So MUCH had changed in the past two years, since I first went to Monsieur Degas's studio to pose for him. Now I was sixteen, no longer a child, a *coryphée* earning one thousand francs a year. This was three hundred francs more than I had earned in the *quadrille,* but it was still not nearly enough to lift our family from poverty.

"Look," Antoinette said, "I give Maman practically all of my wages as it is. Supposedly that money is to go for rent and fuel for the stove, but you know as well as I do what happens to it. I can do nothing more until I find a new patron. Besides, it's Maman's duty, not mine, to take more responsibility for this family."

Antoinette was right, but it hardly mattered. We both understood that Maman was lost to us, her mind addled by drink. Her ritual was familiar: the bitter green liquid in the glass, the spoon with the lump of sugar balanced on the rim, the water poured slowly over the sugar, turning the bright emerald liquid to a milky gray green. As she sipped, her expression changed from weary resignation to dreamy contentment.

But then the contentment drained from her face, and her empty eyes were rimmed with dark circles. "My health is poor," she reminded me often, after insisting that I find a patron. "I'm a dying woman. The day will soon come when the three of you will have only one another."

During these conversations I often thought of my dear papa. What would he have me say to her? Pity and sorrow welled up inside me, but whatever tender feelings I once had for my mother were swept away by a rising tide of anger. I tried to hide my resentment.

"Maman," I begged, "if only you could stop drinking! Surely it's not too late to save yourself."

"I know, I know." Maman sighed deeply. "Your papa would be ashamed of me! I will try to stop, Marie," she said, tears running freely down her haggard cheeks. "I promise."

But I had heard these words and seen those tears many times before, and we both knew this was a promise she could not keep.

———

IF SOMEONE—Monsieur Degas, perhaps, or Mademoiselle Cassatt—had asked me what I wanted my future life to be like, I could have answered easily: "I want to be Jean-Pierre's wife and a *premier sujet* of the Paris Opéra ballet." In my mind it was so simple, so clear! But my mother's drinking and our struggle against poverty made my dreams seem as out of reach as the moon.

The pressure on me to find a patron eased when Antoinette took up with a new gentleman, Lucien Daudet. My sister was pleased with this triumph, and I was relieved to have her mood improve. Lucien was barely twenty, tall and elegantly thin, with ice-blue eyes, dark ringlets, and small black mustaches—a handsome but badly spoiled young man still under his mother's thumb. The Comtesse Daudet doled out Lucien's generous monthly allowance but required him to account for his expenses.

"Down to the last centime," Antoinette pouted. "He's such a baby, but he's adorable, isn't he?"

Antoinette called him her LuLu and petted him as though he were a puppy. But the countess made it impossible for Lucien to court Antoinette in the manner she expected. Instead of getting gifts like the dresses she'd received from Monsieur Chevreul and the jewels and furs she felt she deserved, Antoinette received only tins of candied chestnuts, bouquets of roses and lilacs, and once, a shawl of cream-colored mohair. My sister was scornful of these gifts, and when a few months later she met Paul Hugon—an *abonné* who owned a string

of racehorses and who, she declared, was "rich enough"—
she decided to pass Lucien along to me.

Her audacity left me openmouthed. "You have the nerve
to do this?" I gasped when I managed to speak.

"You're either unable or unwilling to find a wealthy man
on your own," she chided me. "Probably because of that
wretched little stableboy who makes sheep's eyes at you. Oh,
I know all about your Jean-Pierre! And so, *ma petite,* now
that I've at last found myself a mature gentleman with
plenty of francs in his bank account, I'm making you a gift
of our little LuLu."

"You terrible girl!" I cried, still smarting from her spite-
ful reference to the "wretched little stableboy." How dare
she say that! And how had she found out about Jean-Pierre?
"I haven't the slightest interest in 'little LuLu,'" I protested,
"and you know that he has even less interest in me. It's you
he follows around like a trained monkey."

"Just leave it to me," she went on, as though I hadn't spoken, "and you won't have a thing to worry about. It will be
like weaning an infant from its mother's breast. But after
that, it's up to you, Marie," she warned. "You must do your
part. LuLu's a decent enough fellow, and he won't make you
do anything you don't want to do. He might even be relieved
if you refuse his advances, at least for a while. He's still more
boy than man and used to getting his own way. He'll pout at
first when you refuse him, but then he'll understand that he
must woo you, buy you gifts, send you sweets and flowers.

It will be like a game for him and good practice for you. Just remember this bit of advice: If you want something from a man, you must weep for it. And if he wants something from you, you must make him pay for it."

Antoinette, dressing to go out, lovingly unfolded a new pair of silk stockings. "Don't worry, I'll teach you how to manage it all. I'm going after a much bigger prize: persuading Monsieur Hugon to set me up in an apartment of my own, fill my wardrobe with pretty dresses and bonnets and pelisses, hire me a cook and a footman and a maid, and give me an allowance in the bargain."

I stared at my sister as she carefully rolled the costly stocking over her knee, and my frustration seethed to the surface. "How dare you buy yourself silk stockings," I cried, "when Charlotte's underthings are in tatters and her stockings full of holes!"

Antoinette fastened her garter before she answered. "It's the cost of doing business," she said, a hard edge to her voice. "One must present oneself well in order to attract a man of quality. A gentleman is not interested in keeping company with someone whose linens are indecent." She pulled on the second stocking. "I'll give as much as I can to you and Maman and Charlotte, once I've secured Monsieur Hugon's patronage."

She was describing the life of a *lorette*, a kept woman. I knew that *abonnés* who paid extravagant compliments to their favorite dancers were also willing to pay a high price for the privilege of claiming them. I knew, too, that my sister was not the only girl in the Opéra ballet who dreamed that a gentleman in a black silk top hat would pay handsomely for her favors. I was deeply ashamed for Antoinette, but if she felt even the slightest shame herself, she hid it well.

"These are things you must keep in mind with Lucien," she said, smoothing her dress over her hips. "I'll lend you what you need at first, until he starts giving you gifts. But you must be careful of my things." She shook her finger close to my face. "No more boat rides!"

I struggled with a wealth of conflicting feelings. It was clear to me that I must do something. My sister was pushing me into a liaison with Lucien Daudet that, unless I played my cards exactly right, would take me down the same dishonorable path she had chosen. But perhaps I could offer Lucien simple friendship, the kind that existed between Monsieur Degas and Mademoiselle Cassatt, and he would be content with that. Surely such an arrangement was possible, wasn't it? I clung to that notion.

"Suppose Lucien doesn't like me?" I asked. "And what if I can't bear *him*?"

Antoinette was rouging her lips. "He'll adore you. Why wouldn't he? Just be patient and put up with him. His *maman* may croak at any time, and once she does, he'll be able to spend as much as he wants on whomever he wants. It might as well be you."

Indeed, I thought, *it might as well be me. But,* my mind raced on, *what about Jean-Pierre? How will I explain it to him? And what will he think of me?*

But these were not questions I could ask Antoinette.

18

The Empty Case

Jean-Pierre was always on my mind that winter, but we had few chances to be together. Classes, rehearsals, and performances left me little time for pleasure. Jean-Pierre seized a free hour whenever he could, and I'd find him shivering outside the Opéra or huddled in the doorway of the tobacconist's shop below our rooms. We'd link arms and walk fast to keep warm. I couldn't bear to invite him to our cold and dismal rooms, especially if my mother was there. And we couldn't retreat to Jean-Pierre's snug little loft above the stables, because the owner had forbidden employees to bring guests there; the livery was in a neighborhood of prostitutes of the lowest type, and some of them had been caught in the empty horse stalls with their customers.

If we had a few extra *sous* between us, we'd stop at a café and linger over steaming cups of coffee with milk. When we managed to meet during the day, we'd wander through the galleries of the Louvre, gazing at the pictures. Jean-Pierre was most attracted to paintings of horses; I preferred scenes of the sea.

On one of our walks in the early spring as the weather warmed, I noticed posters announcing the Fifth Exhibition of Independent Artists, opening on the first of April. I recognized two of the names: M. Edgar Degas and Mlle Mary Cassatt.

"Are you in his pictures?" Jean-Pierre asked.

"Not in the pictures, but in a sculpture," I replied proudly. "A statuette called *Little Dancer Aged Fourteen.*"

"I'd like to see it," he said, squeezing my hand. "My sweetheart, the famous dancer." He brushed a stray wisp of hair from my face. "Marie, do you think you could teach me to read?"

"*Bien sûr.* We can start right now."

I leaned close to him as we studied the poster together, my other problems pushed well out of mind and my heart singing.

JEAN-PIERRE AND I talked about many things—Monsieur Degas; the Cassatts; Madame Théodore; my friends at the Opéra—but I avoided certain subjects: Maman's drinking; Antoinette's plan to become a *lorette;* and my weakening resolve, born of my desperation, regarding the *foyer de la danse*. I hadn't the courage to hear what Jean-Pierre would say.

Because I could think of no other way to remain a dancer and get the money my family needed, I swallowed my misgivings and went to the *foyer de la danse*. Lucien Daudet promptly took notice of me. He swaggered up, carrying a glass of champagne and smirking. "So," he said, "you must be the mysterious 'little dancer aged fourteen.'"

"I have no notion what you're talking about, Monsieur Daudet," I said, wondering what he knew about the statuette.

His eyes, half closed, gave his handsome features a sleepy, lizardlike appearance. "Your sister told me that you've modeled for Edgar Degas, and that he's been working on a sculpture of you for the past year or so. *C'est vrai, non?*"

"*Oui*, it's true," I acknowledged. "You've seen it, then? The statuette?" I felt a shiver of excitement.

"Not quite," he drawled, sipping his champagne. "Maman and I visited the Fifth Exhibition of Independent Artists last week. My mother finds their work rather droll. In the same little gallery with perhaps a dozen of Degas's dance pictures, which I frankly thought rather silly, plus a few etchings of those two Cassatt sisters, I encountered a great mystery: a vitrine about a meter high, to which was affixed a small brass plaque engraved with a title: PETITE DANSEUSE DE QUATORZE ANS. A lovely glass cabinet, but empty as . . . as"—he searched for the apt words and then lifted his glass and drained the champagne in one swallow—"as this champagne glass!"

"Empty? But where was the statuette?"

Lucien threw up his hands. "Who knows, Mademoiselle? Everyone was talking about it, of course, and it was the object of a good many jokes. Everyone came to stare at the empty case, as though expecting the statuette to appear miraculously before their eyes. The strange sight provoked laughter and a buzz of speculation: *What can it possibly mean? Where's the missing statuette? What kind of trick is Degas up to now?* Luckily your Monsieur Degas wasn't there to hear them! Naturally, since you were the model for this extraordinary work of genius, I felt sure you'd have an explanation."

I was so stunned by this strange news that I could think of no reply. Lucien's face loomed several inches above mine, and he seemed to be enjoying my shock and disappointment.

"I've since heard a rumor," Lucien said with an indolent smile, "that the sculpture no longer exists."

"No longer exists?"

"That he destroyed it. Smashed it so there's nothing left of it but a shapeless lump of wax."

"Destroyed the statuette?" I repeated stupidly. Surely Lucien was lying, having his fun at my expense. Suddenly the knot of anger that had been gathering in the pit of my stomach exploded. I struck out at that simpering smile, the half-closed eyes, and slapped Lucien's face with all my strength. "How dare you say such a thing!"

The smile vanished, Lucien's eyes snapped open wide, and his fingers rose to touch the pale cheek that now bore the bright red imprint of my hand.

Aghast at what I had done, I stepped back, stammering apologies. From the corner of my eye I saw Antoinette staring at me.

"Hellcat," Lucien said at last, attempting a laugh. "The little dancer is actually a hellcat."

"I'm so sorry, Monsieur," I murmured. "Forgive me, I beg you."

"I'll forgive you," he said, his ice-blue eyes darkening. "Provided you'll join me for supper after tonight's performance."

I accepted. I had no choice. If Lucien decided to inform the director of the Opéra that a dancer had actually struck an *abonné*, I would be severely punished—perhaps even dismissed.

Just then, mercifully, the bell rang, and I hurried to my place in the *coulisses* to wait for the curtain to rise on the last act of Meyerbeer's *Robert le diable*. We had performed it many times, but that night I danced poorly. I was worried that Lucien might yet report me, but I was also distracted by his description of the scene at the exhibition: the empty glass case and the mocking laughter. What had happened to the statuette? *My* statuette? I had seen it just weeks before, ready for the costume ordered by Monsieur Degas, waiting for the wig of real hair. He had been putting the finishing touches on the face. *My* face! Had he actually destroyed the *Little Dancer? But why? How could he?*

WHEN ANTOINETTE met me in the dressing room after the performance, I braced myself for a scolding. Amazingly, she said nothing about the incident in the *foyer de la danse*. Her attention was elsewhere. She was in an excellent humor, having just made arrangements to dine with her new conquest, Monsieur Hugon. When I told her that I was to meet Lucien for supper, she looked surprised and then burst out laughing.

"You obviously need no advice from me on how to handle him!" she said. "But you really need to watch that impulsive temper of yours—throwing a new dress in the Seine, slapping a wealthy *abonné* in the face, what next? Really, Marie, not everyone finds that behavior charming."

Then she looked me over and frowned. I had changed into my striped linen skirt—the same one I'd worn one sunny afternoon with Jean-Pierre—and a chemise with a scrap of lace at the neck. "You're not dressed to go to any decent place, but if he tries to take you someplace cheap— le Rat Mort, for instance—it shows he doesn't value you, doesn't respect you."

"Then what should I do?" I asked sullenly. "You set me up for this, you know. It's your fault!"

Sighing, she took off the delicate cream-colored shawl Lucien had given her and draped it around my shoulders and over my chest, in a manner intended to show off my bosom—which I had little of.

"That's better. But don't lose it!" she warned. "And try not to behave like a shrew. A little of that is quite enough."

GENTLEMEN in top hats lounged outside the Opéra, smoking and chatting while they waited for the dancers to change out of their costumes and remove their stage makeup. I found Lucien standing alone. At first he seemed not to recognize me, and I considered simply walking on past him and going straight home. Instead, I placed myself in front of him and forced myself to speak. "*Bonsoir,* Monsieur Daudet."

His pretty face warmed with a lazy smile, and I was relieved that the print of my hand had faded from his cheek. "And a good evening to you, Mademoiselle," he said, bowing. He offered his arm, and I tucked my hand in the crook of his elbow. "I have a coach waiting on the other side," he said, guiding me toward Place de l'Opéra. On the way I glimpsed my sister on the arm of a fat man fairly bursting out of his waistcoat, his yellowish chin whiskers trailing down his starched shirtfront. Could that be Monsieur Hugon? For a moment I almost felt sorry for my sister.

Lucien helped me into a large landau and swung up beside me. Place de l'Opéra was very crowded, as it always was after a performance, and we were forced to wait until some of the carriages ahead of us had collected their passengers and begun to move out onto Boulevard des Capucines. I could think of nothing to say to my companion, and he seemed to be at a loss for words as well.

While we waited in silence for the crowds to clear, I glanced to my left and discovered to my dismay that the Cassatt sisters and their parents sat waiting in the carriage next to ours. They didn't recognize me, but their coachman did. It was Jean-Pierre.

We gazed at each other for a long moment. Surely, I thought, he knew what I was doing with the young man beside me, who had let his hand fall familiarly on my knee. I pressed my lips together to keep them from trembling and tried to send Jean-Pierre a secret message with my eyes: *I would give anything to be sitting by your side.* Tears welled up and began to roll down my cheeks, and I brushed them away. *I would give anything to be anywhere but here with Lucien Daudet.* And remembering Antoinette's advice to forbid even the least familiarity at first, doling out such favors crumb by crumb, I removed Lucien's hand from my knee.

Jean-Pierre raised his gloved hand to his hat brim and gave me the smallest of salutes. The muscles of his jaw clenched tightly. He flicked his whip, and the Cassatts' carriage rolled forward, carrying Jean-Pierre away.

19

Promises

Usually I left it to Jean-Pierre to come looking for me. This time I could not. He had seen me with Lucien, in the landau with the crest of the house of Daudet, and had surely come to certain conclusions about why I was there. I knew that he must feel hurt and betrayed.

The next day after rehearsal I went straight to 13 Avenue Trudaine and spoke to the Cassatts' ruddy-faced porter. He remembered me from my walks with Batty.

"Can you tell me if Mademoiselle Cassatt has gone out in her carriage?" I inquired.

"Why would you be wanting to know that?" the porter asked, looking me over sharply.

"Monsieur Degas has sent me with a message to deliver to her in person," I lied, slipping a small coin into his hand.

Pocketing the coin, he relented. "Mademoiselle Mary is at her studio. Mademoiselle Lydia and Madame Cassatt have gone out. If they follow their usual custom, they'll all be back in time for tea."

That meant Jean-Pierre was driving them, and I now had some notion of when he'd return to the stable. Thanking the porter, I hurried to la Couronne d'Or, the patisserie below Mademoiselle Cassatt's studio, and bought a lovely apricot tart, left from the day before and marked down to a good price. A gentle rain began to fall as I walked in the direction of the railroad station, Gare Saint-Lazare. I had visited the stable with Jean-Pierre only once, and although I remembered that it was near the station, I wasn't sure how to find it.

The rain fell harder, and I took shelter in one of the entrances to the terminal. A number of prostitutes had also gone there for cover, and when a pair of policemen appeared, idly swinging their batons, the girls scattered like startled pigeons, vanishing into the downpour. I, too, ran away.

I wandered aimlessly, searching for the stable. When by luck I found it, my clothes were soaked. The paper in which the tart was wrapped was wet as well, although I'd tried to protect it beneath my shawl. Drenched, I slipped inside the stable, knowing that I was breaking the rules and that I would be in trouble if someone saw me. Escaping the notice of a couple of stable hands who were mucking out the stalls, I crept up the ladder to Jean-Pierre's loft.

I unwrapped the tart and set it on the leather-bound trunk; fortunately, it hadn't suffered much damage. I spread my shawl out to dry, loosened my braid, and combed my wet hair with my fingers. My hair and clothes were still damp when the huge doors of the stable rumbled open and a carriage rolled in. I listened anxiously as Jean-Pierre unhitched the horse and coaxed it into its stall. I heard the spill of oats into a trough, the slosh of water into a pail, and the squeak of carriage wheels, all accompanied by the music of his low whistle. Presently the ladder creaked under his weight, and Jean-Pierre's head appeared.

His look of astonishment when he saw me quickly turned to resentment and anger. "So, Marie," he said, his voice edged with sarcasm, "to what do I owe this honor?"

"Jean-Pierre," I began, nervously licking my lips, "I beg you, listen to me. I can explain. It's not at all what you think."

He hoisted himself up into the loft. His mouth, usually so ready for laughter or for kisses, was pressed in a thin, hard line. "Explain, then. I'm waiting to hear about the gentleman in the fine carriage. Are you his sweetheart, too?"

"*Non, non,* of course not," I said. I tried to describe the *foyer de la danse* and the gentlemen who came there to converse with the dancers. "Antoinette says that Monsieur Daudet is very kind and expects nothing but simple friendship in return for his kindness. All he asks is a dancer's company at supper after the performances. She says he's more of a boy than a man," I added weakly, but I was interrupted by Jean-Pierre's harsh laughter.

"Marie, do you really believe that? I don't! You're only fooling yourself if you do."

I choked back tears. "I must earn money somehow," I said, my voice trembling. "Our situation is truly desperate." And the whole sordid story of our poverty and Maman's drinking came spilling out.

"Then quit, Marie," he said, his tone gentler. He reached for my hand. "Leave the Opéra ballet. You can find other work, I'm sure. You even know how to read! And you'd never have to visit the *foyer de la danse* again, never have to spend another hour with those 'gentlemen,' as you call them."

His suggestion shocked me, and I drew away from him. I thought he understood how important dancing was to me. "Give up the Opéra ballet? Stop dancing? But I love to dance! I've been training for years to be a dancer! And I have talent, even Monsieur Perrot says so! I can't give that up."

"You wouldn't do it even for me? If you loved me, Marie, you'd quit tomorrow."

A chill suddenly came between us, and at first I couldn't answer. Finally I managed to whisper, "And if you loved me, Jean-Pierre, you wouldn't ask me to quit."

For a long time neither of us spoke. Then, slowly, Jean-Pierre reached out and again took my hand. "You're right," he said at last. "I have no right to ask you to stop dancing.

You must do what you love. Even," he added, "if it comes at a price." This time I didn't pull away.

And then he kissed me, and I kissed him, until presently I remembered the apricot tart.

Jean-Pierre cut the tart into wedges, and we bit into the rich fruit and pastry. "As sweet as my love for you," said Jean-Pierre. When there was one piece left, I picked up the knife and cut it in two. I fed one sliver to Jean-Pierre.

"With this, I pledge my love to you," I said solemnly. "I will never betray you with any of the gentlemen from the *foyer de la danse*. This I promise you."

Gravely Jean-Pierre picked up the last sliver of apricot tart and fed it to me. "With this, I pledge my love to you. One day I shall make you my wife, and I shall care for you and cherish you, and you will never once feel that you must become a *lorette*." He was quiet for a moment, lost in thought. "And I further promise that you are free to dance as long as you wish."

After this little ceremony Jean-Pierre and I huddled together in the cramped loft and listened to the horses nickering softly below and the rain drumming on the roof inches above our heads. The chill had disappeared, replaced by a glow of contentment. *This is the happiest I've ever been*, I thought. But even then I wondered if such happiness could last, for I was surrounded by a sea of troubles.

———

SOON SPRINGTIME had again fully embraced Paris. The trees leafed out in every shade of green from delicate to dark. Even in our poor neighborhood pots of flowers crowded balconies and windowsills, and brilliant bursts of pink, red, lavender, and purple appeared in unexpected places.

Being in love changed everything: Colors seemed more vivid, the scent of blossoms seemed even sweeter. Jean-Pierre came by every chance he had; I would rush out to meet him, and we would hurry away together, lost in each other's eyes.

Maman noticed a difference in me. "Ah, Marie," she sighed, in one of her rare sober moments, "how happy it makes me that you seem to have found someone who makes *you* happy! And so much the better that it's that fine young count! Play your cards right, and he'll take good care of you for many, many years. I'm glad you're not like me, running off with the first handsome fellow to charm you with his good looks and sweet words, with scarcely a *sou* in his pocket!"

Antoinette, who was polishing her fingernails with a suede buffer, snorted with laughter. Maman looked from me to Antoinette and back again. "Now you've done it!" I muttered angrily under my breath.

"Am I wrong, then?" asked Maman.

I covered my face with my hands. *What's the use of lying?* I thought. *I might as well tell her the whole truth.* "You're right, Maman," I said, looking directly at her, "I am in love, but not with Comte Daudet. My sweetheart is Jean-Pierre Bordenave, our old neighbor."

Antoinette interrupted before Maman could reply. "A stableboy, Maman! Not even a tailor's apprentice! Can you imagine throwing away a wonderful opportunity with LuLu for *that*?" She didn't try to hide her disgust.

And I didn't try to hide my resentment. "You know nothing of him, Antoinette!" I cried. "He's a coachman, not just a stableboy, and for a rich American family. He may not have wealth or a title, but he's every bit as much a gentleman in his behavior as Lucien—or your Monsieur Hugon!" I added, remembering the fat, bewhiskered man I'd seen at her side.

Maman clucked her tongue. "What a selfish girl you are, Marie!" she said. "If you refuse to think of your family, then at least give some thought to your own future."

"*Oui*, Maman," I replied sullenly.

Antoinette had not had the last word. "I'm sure your stableboy is very nice"—she said *nice* as though it were a fault "but why do you want to waste your time with a nobody when with just a little effort you might come to enjoy a life of luxury?"

"I would not expect you to understand," I said icily.

EVENTUALLY ANTOINETTE and I made peace, choosing to ignore the ugly words that sometimes passed between us. Uncomfortable as I felt at the *foyer de la danse*, I did allow

Antoinette to convince me to go with her, knowing that Lucien would seek me out. There was no reason *not* to go out for supper with him. Even Jean-Pierre had agreed that dining with an *abonné* was not a betrayal.

One evening after we'd finished a late supper of poached chicken breasts and rice, Lucien took my hand and dropped a pair of garnet earrings into the palm.

"Surely these are deserving of a kiss," he said, closing my fingers over the earrings.

I pretended to be taken aback at the suggestion that even such a generous gift entitled him to more than a sincere *merci*, but I did allow him to kiss my hand.

A week later it was a bracelet of fine filigreed silver; the week after that, a brooch studded with tiny pearls; then an amethyst necklace. Each time, I thanked him and offered him my hand to kiss. Each time, I hid the gift in the toe of an old stocking in my wooden trunk, unsure of what to do with it.

Finally I showed Lucien's gifts to Antoinette.

"Oh, what a great joke!" Antoinette cried, holding each piece to the light to examine it. "I do believe that LuLu has his hand in his mother's jewel box!"

"But what should I do with them?" I asked.

"Sell them," she said, trying on the bracelet.

"I can't do that!" I protested. "They're gifts! And what if the countess finds out?"

This didn't worry Antoinette. "LuLu's problem, dear sister—not yours. I can introduce you to a very discreet dealer who will give you a reasonable price for them—not nearly what they're worth, of course, but what does that matter?"

"I can't do that," I said again.

"Go ahead, then, and be stubborn. But you'd better not let Maman find out what you've got here. She'll trade it for a bottle of absinthe in the blink of an eye."

The next time I met Lucien, I made it a point to wear the earrings and bracelet, and tried to persuade him to take them back. He refused. "They're tokens of my love for you, Marie. Surely, you must know that I adore you!"

I didn't dare suggest that the love tokens were really the property of his mother and there would be trouble when she discovered them missing. Worse yet, she would very likely place the blame on me—if she knew that I existed. And even if she didn't know, she could easily discover that, too.

I kept the jewelry a secret from Jean-Pierre. It was an odd situation, having both young men declaring their love for me. My heart and soul belonged to Jean-Pierre, but I confess that Lucien appealed to my mind. Although he gave the impression of complete indolence, he was both intelligent and educated, and he spent his time writing poetry and essays about art and music. Nothing seemed to delight him more than reading his poems aloud to me—poems about gods and goddesses who dwelled on a mountaintop in ancient Greece. I never quite grasped the meaning, even after he had explained it, although I liked the sound of his words.

But as the weeks passed, Lucien plainly expected more from me than just companionship. I did my best to hold him at a distance, to grant him no liberties. When he tried to kiss me, which he did over and over, I pushed him away— gently, never harshly, but firmly. Still, he kept coming back to me. Maybe he regarded me as a challenge.

Meanwhile, I added an opal ring to my collection.

In early June Lucien actually wept as he told me that his mother had made up her mind to take the curative mineral baths at Marienbad, and that he had no choice but to accompany her to Bohemia. From there she planned to follow a leisurely route back to Paris by way of the Swiss Alps.

"I'll be gone for three months!" he cried miserably. "An entire three months that I won't see you, dearest Marie!"

He covered my hands with kisses until I made him stop. "You're behaving like a silly child," I told him. "Of course you must go with your *maman*. I'll be here when you come back."

"You will? Do you promise?"

I tried to laugh off his fervor. "Where else would I be?"

What a relief to have him go! Now I looked forward to a happy summer, free to spend every possible moment with Jean-Pierre.

20

Good-byes

With Lucien gone it was easy to imagine that he might never come back. That was how I allowed myself to be persuaded that the jewelry really did belong to me.

"Certainly it's yours," Antoinette declared when I mentioned it. "No gentleman would demand the return of a gift given to a lady, especially when he's so obviously madly infatuated with her. It's yours to do as you wish, and if I were you, I'd sell a piece or two. Not all of it—you'll want to keep something to wear when you're with him. Otherwise—" She lifted her shoulders in an expressive shrug.

"Otherwise what?"

"He may think you don't appreciate his gifts, and there will be fewer of them."

Antoinette had recently learned that her new admirer, Monsieur Hugon, had found himself in financial difficulties. There were troubles with his investments, his horses were losing their races, he had suffered heavy gambling losses, and now a lawsuit had been brought against him. All of this meant that Monsieur Hugon wasn't nearly as rich as Antoinette once believed. She had decided to get rid of him.

"He's not the only fish in the sea. When the other *abonnés* return from their travels abroad or their summers in the country, I'll have a whole array of admirers to choose from. But you'd better watch your step," she said, wagging a warning finger, "or I may just snatch that adorable LuLu back from you."

I didn't want to think about Lucien and how I would go about balancing his demands for my time, attention, and— probably—favors against my desire to spend every free moment with Jean-Pierre. But lately Maman had been too ill to work more than a few hours a week, and her wages had dwindled to practically nothing. If Antoinette did decide to "snatch" Lucien back as she threatened, I would have to look for a new gentleman who might not be as easy to handle as Lucien. It was more important than ever to find a way to make up for Maman's lost wages.

I decided to visit Mademoiselle Cassatt's studio, hoping that she might be planning another trip abroad and that she might welcome a companion for Batty. After pacing in front of the patisserie to work up my courage, I climbed to the second floor and knocked. Batty responded with his usual hysterical yapping, and Mademoiselle Cassatt opened the door a sliver.

"Ah, Marie, it's you," she said, not opening the door any wider. "Is there something you want?"

"*Oui*, Mademoiselle," I said—uneasily, because she seemed distracted. "I was wondering if you might need me to spend time with Batty."

The door stayed as it was. "*Non, merci,*" she replied. "My father has rented a villa in the country for the season. We leave in a few days. Batty will go with us."

"Oh," I said, swallowing hard, my hopes now dashed.

"I'm sorry, Marie," she said. She must have noticed my distress, for she added, "I wish I could help you, but I can't. My sister has been very ill. We're terribly worried about her. We're hoping the change will help her. Forgive me."

The door closed softly, and I descended the stairs as desolately as though I were descending into a tomb.

OUR ALREADY GRAVE situation worsened. Antoinette's wages barely covered the rent. All of my wages went for food, but still we were often hungry. It was hard to dance well with an empty stomach.

One morning, when I realized that Charlotte was too weak to attend her morning classes at the Opéra, I made a decision. "Tell me how to find the jewelry dealer," I said to Antoinette.

That same day I took the pearl brooch to a cramped and gloomy shop in a dank little passage on *la rive gauche,* not far from Tante Hélène's dressmaking shop. The dealer offered me twenty-five francs for the brooch.

"That's all?" I asked. "I'm sure it's worth at least twice that."

"Then find another buyer," the dealer said disdainfully. He turned back to his worktable, leaving the brooch on the counter.

I knew no other buyer, and so reluctantly I accepted his offer. That night we feasted on pigeon pie and radishes. When Maman asked where I had gotten the money for the food, I lied: "Jean-Pierre gave it to me." Antoinette studied her polished fingernails and said nothing.

I managed the remaining francs carefully, depositing them in the tin under the tobacconist's counter and withdrawing only a few *sous* at a time. The once cheerful Monsieur Lerat now had little to say. Each time I went to his shop he looked more despondent than the time before. His two little boys raced noisily through the tiny shop, ignoring their father's pleas for quiet. I could think of nothing to say to make him smile, as he had once made *me* smile.

For the next few weeks we ate well. The color came back to Charlotte's cheeks, and I ordered her a new skirt and chemise. Antoinette persuaded me to loan her two francs to buy lace and ribbons for her rose mousseline dress, and a new parasol to replace the one I'd lost in the lake. "Consider it an investment in our future," she said. I knew I'd never see those two francs again.

By summer's end the twenty-five francs was gone. I visited the dealer again, this time with the filigree bracelet. A few weeks later Lucien and the countess returned to Paris.

HAVING LUCIEN BACK in Paris meant the end of my easy times with Jean-Pierre. Lucien again demanded much of my attention, and I felt so guilty for having sold the brooch and bracelet that I believed I was duty bound to spend time with him. Antoinette declared this idea nonsense: "You have no need to feel guilty about anything, ever," she said. But that didn't change my feelings.

In the autumn all three of us once again passed our dance examinations, although none of us received a promotion, and Antoinette got a reprimand from Monsieur Perrot, the ballet master, for her habitual lateness and frequent absences from classes and rehearsals.

"Old windbag!" she fumed, pale with anger, as we were walking home afterward—slowly, because Maman had dragged herself out of bed to accompany us and now could scarcely keep up with us. "Fined me five additional francs on top of the fines I'd already paid—this for what he calls my 'lack of discipline'—and then delivered the ultimatum in front of all the *petits sujets:* 'No more absences or you're finished!' he said. As though I give a snap!" But her trembling voice gave her away; she cared more than she would admit. There was no lunch celebration that day.

Antoinette had proceeded with her plan to rid herself of Monsieur Hugon, and most of her efforts were now going into finding a new patron. No sooner would she meet a gentleman who seemed suitable than she would discover some fault in him and move on. For a time she was juggling the attentions of several *abonnés*.

"Will you make good on your threat to take LuLu back?" I asked one afternoon.

"That depends. How is the countess's health?" she retorted with a wicked grin. I knew that LuLu wouldn't really interest her until he came into his mother's fortune, and the countess was apparently as robust as ever.

I reported this conversation to Jean-Pierre. He laughed, but his laughter sounded hollow, and I knew he was shocked. He didn't much like Antoinette, whom he called "the fortune hunter." I hoped he didn't think the same of me and truly understood that I was forced to accept Lucien's favors.

GREAT BLASTS OF bitter wind swept down from the north. Dry leaves danced in the streets, making whispery sounds. The skies darkened. I drew my shawl over my head and was grateful for the gloves Jean-Pierre had given me the winter before.

Two days before Christmas we heard a knock at the door
and assumed the worst—that the rent collector had come,
or that we were about to be served with a notice of money
owed or a rule broken. "Be quiet," Maman whispered.
"Don't answer it."

But the knocking continued, and a voice came through
the keyhole: "Marie! Marie, are you there?"

I recognized Jean-Pierre's voice and opened the door.
"Thank God I found you," he said. "I have to talk to you,
Marie. Right now—it's important." He looked upset and
half frozen as well.

"Wait for me downstairs," I said, for I still couldn't bring
myself to invite him into our wretched rooms.

I found the army coat that my sisters and I shared and
hurried down to meet him. It was snowing hard.

"Where can we go?" he asked, wet flakes clinging to his
eyelashes.

I had an idea: "To the church."

We hurried through the swirling snowflakes to Notre-
Dame de Lorette and stepped inside. No light streamed
through the high windows that day; dozens of flickering
candles provided the only illumination in the vast, shadowy
sanctuary. A few people were scattered among the seats;
some knelt in prayer, eyes fixed on the crucified Christ above
the altar, while others sat hunched over, wrapped in their
own misery. Two workmen perched on ladders, hanging

greens for the Christmas Eve Mass. We wandered down the side aisles, past murky chapels honoring various saints, and stopped finally at the Lady Chapel.

I could no longer stand the suspense. "What is it, Jean-Pierre? Tell me."

"My father has fallen ill," he said, his voice husky. "My mother sent word with a neighbor, begging me to come to Rouen."

I gripped his hands. "Oh, Jean-Pierre," I sighed. "I am so sorry."

"She can't manage the farm alone. She needs my help. I must go. There's no other way."

"When do you leave?" I asked, my heart wrenched and already aching.

"Tomorrow."

"And when will you come back?" I whispered, fearing the answer. Numbness crept through my arms to my fingertips.

"I don't know," he said. "If my father recovers, I'll be back as soon as he's well enough to let me go. If he does not, then I must stay and help my mother."

"Have you told the Cassatts?"

"Not yet. I wanted to tell you first." He wiped his eyes. "Marie," he said, clearing his throat, "you know that you're my sweetheart, and I love you with all my heart. Will you wait for me? I *will* come back, I promise you."

"*Bien sûr,* I'll wait for you, Jean-Pierre," I said. I didn't think about what I was promising, and that weeks, even months, might pass before I saw him again. There would be no letters, because neither of us had learned to write yet. I didn't think of the pain our separation would bring. I thought only of the love I felt for him.

We sat for a long time in the chapel before the statue of Our Lady, whispering to each other of our love. Old women shuffled in and out, lighting candles, murmuring prayers. A priest walked by briskly, and cast an appraising glance at the two of us huddled together, our fingers tightly laced. I tried not to weep, for Jean-Pierre's sake.

Jean-Pierre reached inside his shirt, pulled out the thin chain with the tiny Saint Christophe medal, kissed it, and hung it around my neck. "Whatever happens," Jean-Pierre said, "I'll come for you, and we'll be married."

"And I will be true to you," I vowed, my fingers on the medal, which was still warm from his body.

The snow was already ankle-deep by the time we left the church. When we reached Rue de Douai, I asked Jean-Pierre to wait while I ran up to our rooms. I dug to the bottom of my wooden trunk for the sketch Monsieur Degas had made of me—the one Antoinette had stolen—refolded it carefully, and carried it downstairs to give to Jean-Pierre. "A souvenir to remember me by."

We kissed one last time, and Jean-Pierre went away.

Paris, 1881

21

The Exhibition

G ood!" exclaimed Antoinette when I told her that Jean-
Pierre had left for his family's farm in Rouen. "Now
maybe you'll forget about him and devote your attention
to LuLu. You've been toying with the poor fellow for
months, and I don't know how much longer you can get
away with your pretense of virtue. He's not likely to hand
over any more of the countess's pretty jewelry if he's not
receiving anything in return. Or am I wrong about all of
this? Have you been LuLu's mistress all along, as well as the
stableboy's?"

"There are times when I truly despise you, Antoinette," I
said coldly. "This is one of those times. The answer is, I've
been neither."

For days I refused to say another word to her, until she apologized—in a way. "I'm sorry if you took offense at what I said, Marie," she said. "But it's hard for me to believe that anyone is as good as you pretend to be."

"I'm not pretending anything."

THERE WAS NOW a large hole in my life. I missed Jean-Pierre terribly. I fingered the tiny Saint Christophe medal that hung between my breasts and longed for him, wondering if he gazed at the sketch I'd sent with him and longed for me as well. At night I lay in bed, hearing Monsieur Degas's folk song in my head, but replacing *Robin* with Jean-Pierre's name: *Jean-Pierre loves me, Jean-Pierre's mine* . . .

To escape the loneliness, I devoted myself to my dancing, and earned words of praise from Madame Théodore and even Monsieur Perrot. Sometimes I went to le Rat Mort with Geneviève, Léonie, and Mathilde, all of whom were now *coryphées,* like me. Around the time of my seventeenth birthday, in February, a new cabaret opened called le Chat Noir—the Black Cat—and my friends invited me to join them there for a little celebration. I accepted, although I was in no mood to celebrate.

The cabaret had three large rooms and a zinc bar in the front salon, which opened onto Boulevard de Rochechouart. There were also a number of private alcoves in the back. It was already crowded and noisy when we arrived, and we searched for a table, finding one that happened to be near a group of dancers. Antoinette was among them. My friends talked of the next round of dance examinations coming in April—they believed I might be promoted to *petit sujet*—and of the gentlemen they'd met at the *foyer de la danse*. The *foyer* had become a way of life for them. They found it exciting.

"You must tell us about Monsieur Daudet!" Léonie insisted. "He's very handsome! Do his mustaches tickle?"

"You're so lucky, finding a young *abonné*," Mathilde sighed. "Most of the men who come to the *foyer de la danse* are old and flatulent and not at all amusing, but Lucien Daudet isn't like that."

"I suppose not," I said, trying to think of a way to change the subject.

"Are you in love with him, then? Are you his mistress?" It was Geneviève, leaning close and asking too many questions, as usual.

"*Mais non,* I'm not, and I'm not going to be," I said. "But I don't want to talk about him."

"*Non?* But why not, Marie? He's such a prize! Those eyes! That mouth!"

Antoinette had apparently been eavesdropping. "Well, I can tell you why," she said, inviting herself to join our table. "She's pining for a stableboy who hasn't the price of the cheapest seat for a single night, and who has furthermore left Paris *supposedly* to care for his ailing mother. Or is it his papa?"

"Shut up, Antoinette," I muttered, hating the way she'd slyly emphasized *supposedly*. "Jean-Pierre is worth ten of Lucien Daudet."

But Antoinette was drinking wine, and her tongue was loose. "Can you imagine? My sister doesn't deserve to have LuLu chasing after her. I'm betting that I can take him away from her whenever I want, just like that!" She snapped her fingers and winked at me. "Isn't that so, Marie?"

"Then take him," I retorted. "But remember that the Comtesse Daudet seems to be in excellent health, and your LuLu is no closer than he ever was to receiving his inheritance."

To the sound of my friends' raucous laughter, Antoinette removed herself to a different table.

FOR SEVERAL NIGHTS there was no sign of Lucien at the Opéra, which was unusual, for he rarely missed a performance. Then word spread through the *foyer de la danse* that the Comtesse Daudet had been taken by apoplexy and had died within hours.

Almost immediately a rumor began to circulate: Lucien had promised his mother, as she drew her last breath, that after a period of mourning he would marry Émilie Bosc, the youngest daughter of a wealthy art dealer with galleries in London and New York.

Could this be true? None of us knew whether to believe

it or not. Antoinette reacted as though she'd been stung by a hornet. "What a horror! We're finally rid of the old countess, only to have her place taken by a young bride! It will be years before our LuLu is his own man."

I felt nothing but relief. If Lucien had a wife, I would no longer have to endure his unwelcome advances. Soon, though, I would have to look for a new patron or find another source of money.

POSTERS BEGAN TO appear in neighborhoods around the Palais Garnier, advertising the April opening of the Sixth Exhibition of Independent Artists. Again I recognized the names of Monsieur Degas and Mademoiselle Cassatt. Although Monsieur Degas was always visible in the classrooms and *coulisses*, he had not spoken a word to me in months. What had happened to the statuette? A year ago Lucien had told me that Monsieur Degas had destroyed it, smashed it so that there was nothing left but a shapeless lump of wax. Had Monsieur Degas begun all over again, finished the statuette at last, dressed it in its tutu and slippers? Would *Petite danseuse* appear in this exhibition? The one person who might be able to tell me was Lucien.

Not long after the opening of the exhibition, Lucien put in his first appearance at the Opéra since the countess's death. He came to the *foyer de la danse* wearing a black ribbon in the buttonhole of his coat, in place of his usual gardenia. I offered him my condolences, which he acknowledged somberly. Then he asked me to accompany him to supper after the performance. I accepted.

His landau—formerly the countess's carriage—was draped in black crepe. We drove to a quiet café, away from the crowds, near Place de l'Opéra and ordered a meal of braised duckling. I listened respectfully while Lucien spoke of his mother, the suddenness of her death, the magnificence of the funeral, his nearly overwhelming grief now that she was gone. There was no mention of a coming marriage.

"I shall devote my life to writing," he said with a tremor in his voice. "I intend to dedicate a book of my poems to my mother's memory." He pulled out a handkerchief embroidered with the family crest and dabbed at his eyes. I agreed that his poems would do the countess great honor.

As the meal progressed, Lucien's mood seemed to lighten a little, and I tried to think of a way to ask if he had seen the exhibition. Then Lucien himself introduced the subject.

"You're quite famous now, you know," he said, digging a spoon into an apple custard. "Everyone is talking about Monsieur Degas and *Petite danseuse de quator\e ans*. Several days after the exhibition opened, once again with an empty case, the statuette suddenly appeared. It has turned the Paris art world on its head! Surely you must have heard?"

"*Mais non*, I have not," I told Lucien. "I haven't posed for Monsieur Degas in almost a year." *What wonderful news*, I thought; *he finished it after all!* "So you've seen it then?"

"I have. He destroyed it, but then he restored it to life—an artist's privilege. It's extraordinary. No sculptor has ever done anything like it: He dressed the statuette in real clothes and smeared a thin layer of hot wax over all of it, making the tights and bodice and slippers part of the sculpture itself. Then he added the gauze tutu and a wig made of real hair, a single braid just like yours, tied with a green ribbon."

As Lucien described the statuette, I grew more and more excited. I knew that I had to see it.

Lucien hailed a waiter and ordered a glass of cognac for himself and a coffee for me. "I've been invited to write a review of the exhibition for an arts journal," he said. "I'm not sure what I'll write about *Petite danseuse*. Some claim it's a masterpiece, but most others say it's a scandal. People either love it or hate it. There is no in-between."

"And what do *you* say, Lucien?" I asked.

"*Ma chère* Marie, it looks just like you. And I adore you, of course." He leaned closer, smiling, reaching for my hand.

"Lucien," I said, letting my hand rest in his, "I must see the statuette. Take me to the exhibition, I beg you."

"But that's out of the question, Marie," he said, releasing my hand, his smile replaced by a frown. "You know as well as I that only people of a certain class visit the galleries. I'd be a laughingstock if I showed up there with the model!"

"No one will know. I'll borrow one of Antoinette's dresses and her bonnet, and once we're inside you can pretend you don't know me," I pleaded, refusing to be put off.

"It might be rather amusing," he said, relenting at last and promising to take me the following day.

AFTER REHEARSAL I rummaged through Antoinette's wardrobe until I found a modest dress of gray watered silk. I fastened the amethyst necklace Lucien had given me and borrowed Antoinette's rouge for my lips. With one of her bonnets my transformation was complete, and I set off to meet Lucien on Boulevard des Capucines.

I was grateful to find him waiting for me in his landau. He offered me his arm and escorted me into the gallery, as though I were a wellborn lady. I was so nervous and excited that I had to remind myself to take deep breaths, as I did when I was preparing to make an entrance onstage.

Lucien steered me quickly from room to room. As we passed the paintings that hung on the walls, I recognized some by Mademoiselle Cassatt, including the painting of her sister Lydia in the striped chair, holding a teacup—maybe even the same teacup I once held in my own hand. Several well-dressed ladies and gentlemen were admiring lovely pictures of mothers with plump babies who glowed with good health.

A noisy crowd had gathered in the last of the exhibition rooms, where Monsieur Degas's familiar pictures of laundresses and dancers were displayed. But the crowd ignored the pictures, pressing close to a glass case in the center of the room.

"There she is," Lucien whispered into my ear. "Or perhaps, better to say, 'There you are.' *Little Dancer Aged Fourteen.*"

I worked my way to the front of the throng until I was standing next to the glass case. I'd approached the statuette from the side, rather than face-to-face. The sensation was like none I had ever experienced. My heart began to pound as I gazed at the figure in the vitrine. I felt as though my soul had escaped and was now seeing my body from the outside. That statuette seemed as real, as alive, as I was.

No one noticed me standing beside them in the borrowed dress and bonnet. They stared with rapt attention at the statuette. Some of them laughed. All around me, voices babbled: *Why is she so ugly? . . . She looks vicious! More like a little monkey than a little girl! . . . If she were smaller one would be tempted to pickle her in a jar! . . . Heaven forbid that my daughter should become a dancer and end up like that!*

The terrible voices tore at me, clawed at my stomach, slapped my face, yanked my hair. But, then, other voices joined the clamor: *Magnificent! . . . Look at her! There's nothing like it in modern sculpture . . . Degas is a genius. He's given us a new kind of beauty.*

I felt faint. The room began to spin, and my legs weakened and buckled beneath me as the voices continued their gibbering. Luckily, Lucien caught me as I fell. When I woke up I was lying on the seat of his landau, Lucien's worried face peering down at me.

"Are you all right, Marie?" he asked.

I nodded. "She's so real," I murmured, sitting up. "And they scorn her because they think she's ugly."

"Those who scorn her do so because they don't understand true beauty. Come, I'll get you something to eat. Perhaps you'll feel better."

TWO CHEESE TARTS arrived, and I devoured mine hungrily. Lucien left his tart untouched, watching me. When I had finished, he threw down his napkin and leaned forward, his eyes searching mine. "I have an important question to ask you, Marie. Will you be my mistress? I'm now in a position to set you up in a style that I think you'll find quite rewarding. Say you will!"

I wasn't expecting this, and his proposal caught me off guard. "But what about Mademoiselle Bosc? I've heard that you're engaged to be married!"

"The one has nothing to do with the other, *ma chère* Marie. I'm no longer a mere boy, you know. I am a man! In the past you've always turned me away, but things are different now."

"Different for you, perhaps, but not for me. I can't be your mistress—not now, not ever."

Lucien claimed to be a man, but he reacted like a boy. First he pouted. Then he whined and begged. When I couldn't tolerate any more, I thanked him for taking me to the exhibition, thanked him for his friendship, expressed again my sorrow for his bereavement, and wished him well in his coming marriage. And then I left the café, not waiting for him to drive me home. I wasn't thinking of Lucien as I climbed toward Rue de Douai, but of *Petite danseuse*. Why were people laughing at her? Was she truly ugly? Was *I*?

I could not let go of the image of the statuette that seemed more real than not. Nor could I erase the sound of those hateful voices: *Ugly . . . vicious . . . monkey . . . Heaven forbid that my daughter should become a dancer and end up like that!* I hoped that the glass case protected the *Little Dancer* from those harsh, unfeeling voices. And what about Monsieur Degas? Did the voices hurt him as much as they hurt me? Or was he able to ignore them?

I longed to tell Jean-Pierre about the statuette and the things people were saying about it, and to let him comfort me, but that was impossible. He had been gone for four months, and I had to assume that his papa had not recovered and that Jean-Pierre had to stay in Rouen at least through the spring planting season.

The one person in Paris who might truly understand my feelings was Lucien, but my refusal to become his mistress had undoubtedly ended whatever friendship we might have had. I'd never felt so alone.

22

Le Chat Noir

Three days after Lucien took me to see the statuette, I watched Antoinette put on her finest dress of pale blue and white foulard, and her best silk stockings and garters.

"For whose benefit is this?" I asked; I hadn't seen her so elegantly dressed since the days of Monsieur Hugon.

She stopped fixing her hair long enough to smile at me. "Comte Daudet."

I wished I'd been able to disguise my shock, but I could not. "Lucien?" I gasped.

"*Bien sûr!* I told you that the moment you decided you'd had enough of LuLu—or the other way around—I would happily take him back. And I have!" She drew a thin black line of kohl across each eyelid and stood back to admire the effect in our speckled mirror. "There was nothing to it! LuLu was ripe for the plucking, having just lost his dear *maman*. Poor lamb, he's engaged to a very cold woman—I'm sure his Émilie has ice water in her veins—and he knows exactly where to turn for warmth in his life."

Only days earlier he'd told me that he adored me. Was it really possible for a man to shift his affections so quickly? There was nothing I could say—I hadn't told Antoinette of Lucien's offer to make me his mistress, nor had I mentioned our visit to the exhibition—and I had no intention of telling her now. "Where are you going with him?" I asked.

"Le Chat Noir. I imagine he'll find it exciting, don't you?" She was dabbing a cheap cologne behind her ears.

"I suppose," I said sullenly.

Antoinette pinned on a velvet toque with a glossy black feather, and buttoned her gloves. *"Au revoir, chère* Marie,*"* she trilled, waggling her fingers at me. Her boots tapped smartly down the stairs.

I WAS ALONE. Charlotte had gone to visit one of her friends, and Maman, who'd been feeling somewhat stronger, was no doubt drinking with the other laundresses at le Rat Mort. I wandered restlessly through our bleak rooms, nearly overcome with despair. Then an idea struck me: Why not go to le Chat Noir myself? Perhaps Mathilde or one of the other *coryphées* might be there, and I might be distracted by the entertainment. If Lucien and Antoinette saw me there, so much the better. It was even possible that my sister was inventing the whole story just to annoy me.

Without a qualm, I borrowed the same gray watered-silk dress from Antoinette's wardrobe and set out, choosing a route past 13 Avenue Trudaine. My heart leaped when I saw the Cassatts' carriage drawn up in front of the building, but I soon realized that the coachman in the top hat was a wizened old man in a threadbare coat, and not my Jean-Pierre. This wasn't the first time I thought I'd glimpsed my sweetheart. Naturally, I was always disappointed.

I strolled past the entrance of le Chat Noir, but there was no sign of the landau with the Daudet crest. I slipped in through a side entrance and found a small table in a poorly lit corner from which I could observe the crowd and search for my friends. I saw a few dancers from the Opéra, but they were *premiers sujets* and would not have welcomed my company. There was no sign of Mathilde or any *coryphées*. A waiter with waxed mustaches took my order for a plate of oysters and a glass of Vichy water.

Even before the oysters arrived, I spotted Antoinette and Lucien making their way through the large dining room toward one of the private alcoves. I bowed my head so that the bonnet hid my face and peeped out to watch them disappear behind a heavy velour curtain.

I barely tasted the oysters, keeping an eye on the velour

curtain and listening to occasional bursts of my sister's lilting laughter and Lucien's mellow baritone. The lights dimmed and the entertainment began: Magic-lantern slides of ancient ruins projected onto a screen while a piano provided musical accompaniment. The music had built to a dramatic crescendo when suddenly a commotion broke out in the alcove. His waistcoat unbuttoned, Lucien emerged, shouting, "Police! Thief! Police! Thief!"

In a moment the owner of the establishment appeared and tried to calm Lucien, who continued to cry out that he had been robbed. The owner plunged behind the velour curtain, and when a pair of gendarmes arrived, they, too, followed the distraught Lucien behind the curtain.

I heard a shriek and half rose from my seat, unsure if I should rush to help my sister or stay where I was. Other customers, ignoring the images on the screen, had turned to stare at the drama unfolding on the other side of the room. Even the pianist stopped playing and watched.

My legs weak and shaking, I nearly collided with the gendarmes, who emerged from the alcove after much angry shouting, half dragging Antoinette. "What's happening?" I cried. "What are they doing to her?"

Her velvet toque askew, Antoinette struggled to maintain her dignity, loudly insisting, "There must be some mistake, Officers, I'm sure Monsieur Daudet is mistaken; nothing is amiss . . ."

All the while, Lucien, white with rage, was exclaiming, "She tried to steal my money, the tart! Took my purse from my waistcoat pocket and slipped most of my money into her stocking! I demand that you arrest her!"

Tossing a few coins down next to my unfinished oysters, I rushed out of the cabaret by the side door as the two gendarmes shoved Antoinette, who was weeping angrily, into their police wagon. The flounces of her dress were half torn off, her toque now missing entirely. A third police officer took Lucien aside and began to make notes on a pad as Lucien spoke, waving his arms in agitation. The third officer patted Lucien's shoulder consolingly and swung up beside the driver of the police wagon as the wagon lurched off down Boulevard de Rochechouart.

Trembling, I knelt and picked up the little velvet toque. The glossy black feather was crushed, and I tried futilely to straighten it. Lucien stumbled toward his landau, the heels of his hands pressed against his temples. Then he noticed me standing there, clutching Antoinette's hat and too frightened to move or to speak.

"Ah, so it's you, Marie! Your sister is a thief. She tried to rob me," he said tonelessly. "Filched my purse from my pocket"—he touched his breast, where the purse had been—"and emptied it of six hundred francs. I hardly knew what had happened." He shook his head slowly, in disbelief. "I trusted her, as I trusted you," he muttered. "What a fool

I am. To hell with both of you!" He climbed into his carriage and ordered the coachman to drive him home.

"Where are they taking her?" I shouted after Lucien, tears streaming down my face. "What will happen to her?"

But Lucien clattered away without a backward glance.

In a panic I left le Chat Noir and rushed home. Charlotte was there, sleeping soundly. Unable to think clearly, I shook her awake. "Where's Maman?"

Charlotte gazed up at me drowsily. "Don't know," she said, but the alarm in my voice roused her fully. "What happened?" she asked. "What's wrong?"

"It's Antoinette. She's in trouble." I described the scene, trying to make it sound as though it had all been a misunderstanding, a terrible mistake.

"Where did they take her?" asked Charlotte, her gray eyes huge.

"I don't know." I had begun pacing, wringing my hands.

"Then we must find her," Charlotte said resolutely, already pulling on her clothes.

I began to argue that she must not come with me, that she was too young to be exposed to this sordid scene, but I was so frightened and upset—and Charlotte so determined—that in the end I relented.

It was very late when Charlotte and I set out for the police station in the Ninth Arrondissement. The churlish gendarme on duty gave us no information, except to say in a bored voice that Antoinette had no doubt been sent off "to get what she deserves."

"Where would that be, sir?" I asked politely—although I yearned to squeeze his thick neck until he turned blue.

"Try the magistrate's court," he said. "And you'd best mind your manners, you little tramps, or you'll wind up like your sister."

Charlotte, unused to being spoken to so rudely, flinched as though the gendarme had struck her. I threw the man a hateful look and led Charlotte away.

WE DIDN'T FIND Antoinette that night. Soon after we'd returned home, exhausted and disheartened, Maman arrived, somewhat addled from drink. When she heard my story, she was furious—both at Lucien Daudet for having my sister arrested, and at Antoinette for getting caught—and began to shout drunkenly that no doubt Comte Daudet had set a trap for her innocent daughter. "He'll pay for this!" she ranted, seizing a kitchen knife and brandishing it. "I'll have my revenge!"

"She's gone mad," Charlotte whispered to me.

"It's the serpent with green eyes," I said quietly. "Go to bed, Charlotte. I'll calm her."

Obediently Charlotte lay down and drew the ragged quilt over her head. I spoke soothingly to Maman, persuading her to relinquish the knife, and at last got her to lie down, too.

Soon both Charlotte and Maman had drifted into an uneasy slumber. I sat through the remainder of the night, unable to sleep, worrying and praying: *What should I do? What can I do?*

It was during the hour just before dawn, while the sky was dark and starless, that I thought I heard my dear papa speak to me, in almost the same way he had spoken the week before he died. He reminded me of the promise I had made to hold our family together.

Marie, I imagined him whispering, *your sisters need you more than ever. Your mother is lost, I'm afraid. Do what you can to help Antoinette—she's not a bad girl, just a good girl gone down the wrong path. But above all, save the baby . . . Charlotte . . . you must save Charlotte . . .*

Again I laid my hand on my heart and promised: *Oui, mon cher* Papa. *I will do all that I can.*

I felt him kiss my cheek—and my eyes flew open. Had I been dreaming? It seemed so real, but there was no one there, just the sound of my sister's sighing and my mother's drunken snore.

23

Prison Saint-Lazare

The morning after Antoinette's arrest, I awakened Charlotte. We left without trying to rouse Maman, who was still sunk in a stupor. When we reached the street, I hugged Charlotte and sent her off to the Opéra with a message for Madame Théodore.

"Tell her it's a family emergency, and I can't come to class this morning. If she asks if I'll be at the afternoon rehearsal, say that you don't know. And don't say anything at all about Antoinette."

"But where are you going, Marie?" Charlotte asked, clinging to me.

"To find Antoinette. Don't worry," I said, kissing her again. *I* would do the worrying for both of us.

I had been frightened and distraught when my sister was

dragged away by the gendarmes the night before. But this morning I was angry, outraged that Antoinette had done something so stupid, so foolish, so *wrong!* What had she been thinking? Didn't she realize the risk she was taking, putting herself and her family in jeopardy? But angry as I was I had to find out what had happened and what lay in her future— and in ours.

There was no time to lose. Missing the morning class and afternoon rehearsal would cost me a stiff fine, but if I missed the performance that night I would also get a black mark on my record. Besides that, the spring dance examinations were coming up in less than a week.

After hours of what seemed fruitless searching and questioning unsympathetic clerks, I learned that my sister had been jailed in the women's prison called Saint-Lazare— about a half-hour's walk from our home. Dark and forbidding, Saint-Lazare had once been a hospital for lepers, and now mostly housed prostitutes convicted of other crimes. Despite pleading with an insolent matron at the prison, I was not permitted to visit Antoinette, and by the time I rushed to the Opéra I was too late for the evening performance. I avoided Madame Théodore and the other dancers, and found Charlotte sitting alone on a bench backstage, her head buried in her hands.

"Everyone is talking about Antoinette," Charlotte said, miserably. "They know about her. Somebody saw the gendarmes take her away."

"It's all right," I lied, my arms around her. "I'll see her to-morrow. Everything will be fine."

THE NEXT DAY, Sunday, I rose early and set off for the prison. With hordes of others who had come to visit the prisoners, I was kept waiting outside the iron gates for most of the day. When the gates at last swung open, the guard shouted a warning: In one hour the gates would be locked again, and anyone caught inside would be treated as a pris-oner. Shuddering, I stumbled through dank corridors, some-times losing my way. Moisture seeped through the stone walls. The stench was horrible, and the unearthly wailing and screeching of the inmates raised the fine hairs on the back of my neck.

I found Antoinette crouched in a filthy cell with several other girls and women of all ages, each dressed in shapeless, dun-colored smocks and soiled linen caps. At first I didn't recognize my sister. Her face was smudged, her beautiful eyes ringed with exhaustion.

"Oh, Marie, thank God you've come!" she cried when she saw me. "You can't believe what a miserable place this is! Look, they've cut off my hair!" She pulled off the cap to re-veal straggly locks of blond hair, crudely chopped above the ears. "Have you brought me anything to eat? I'm famished! What they give us is no better than the slops you'd feed a pig." She gripped the iron bars of the cell and pressed her face against them.

During the hours I had searched for Antoinette, I swore that when I found her I would demand that she admit her guilt and swear that she was sorry. But she looked so wretched that Papa's words from my dream echoed in my head—*not a bad girl, just a good girl gone down the wrong path*—and I reached out to touch her forehead and her chin in an attempt to comfort her. Instead of accusing her, I asked, "What happened after the police took you away? How long will you be kept here?"

Antoinette cursed. "The magistrate sentenced me to three months," she groaned. "I can't survive for three months in this dreadful hole!"

"Three months!" I exclaimed. "But what's going to happen? You'll be dismissed from the Opéra—surely you know that!"

"You'll talk to them, won't you, Marie? To Monsieur Perrot? They'll take me back, I'm sure of it."

"How can you believe such a thing?" I exclaimed.

Antoinette burst into tears, her body shaking with sobs. I had hardly ever seen her cry like that; her tears were almost always a means to get her own way. "Oh, Marie, what am I to do? I'll die here if you don't help me, Marie!"

"All right," I said. "I'll bring what I can."

"There's just one hour in the afternoon for visitors," she said. "Don't bring too much at one time." She glanced over her shoulder and whispered, "These wenches have no scruples. They'd steal the pennies from a dead man's eyes."

At that moment the prison matron strode through the gloomy passageway, shouting, "Time's up! Time's up!"

"Watch out for her," Antoinette hissed. "She's a mean one."

"Before I go," I whispered hurriedly, "tell me this: Is it true what Lucien has accused you of, that you're a thief?"

"Ugh, that LuLu!" she spat. "What a hateful boy! I took some money from him, but he has so much and we have so little, I don't understand why he's so upset. He could have simply asked me to return the money and I would have done it. He didn't need to put up such a fuss, calling the police, as though I'm a common criminal."

"Time's up! Time's up!" the prison matron again shouted.

"But it was wrong, Antoinette! And now you're in prison, and all of us are being punished. How are we to survive without your wages?"

Antoinette reached through the bars of the cell and gripped my fingers. "I'm sorry to be causing you so much trouble," she said, sounding contrite. "I'll make it all up to you, just as soon as I get out of here. I'll pay you back, I swear."

I didn't believe her promises. I tried to pull away. "I'll come back when I can. You know I have no money."

She tightened her grip. "On the top shelf of the pantry, all the way in the back. The little leather purse." So that's where she'd hidden it! "Tomorrow, Marie!" she pleaded.

Tomorrow would be my second missed rehearsal and possibly another missed performance. Her voice echoed as I rushed down the corridor. "Marie, tomorrow, I beg you!"

LATER THAT AFTERNOON I found Charlotte hunched in a forlorn heap on our bed. "Where's Maman?" I asked, sitting down beside her.

Charlotte shook her head, her lip trembling. "I don't know. She said she was going out to buy some bread, but she hasn't come back. She said she couldn't stand to stay here and worry about Antoinette."

"Have you had anything to eat?"

"Coffee," she said. "That's all."

I searched the top shelf of the pantry until I found Antoinette's purse. It contained seven francs, plus a few centimes. I took it all. "Come, Charlotte," I said. "We'll get something to eat."

We made our way to the Café de la Nouvelle-Athènes, where we found that a festive crowd was gathered. When I remarked on the women's fine silk dresses and bonnets and the men's top hats, Charlotte reminded me reproachfully that it was Easter. I had forgotten. Perhaps we should have gone to le Rat Mort, where I would not have felt so ashamed of our ragged clothes, but I guessed that Maman might be there, and I was in no mood to see her. A waiter passed by, bearing a tray of food that smelled indescribably delicious. I saw the look of yearning on Charlotte's face and decided that we would stay, shabby or not.

We shared an eel pie and a plate of sliced melon, but I had no appetite and after only a few bites left the rest of my portion untouched. Charlotte ate hungrily while asking me questions about Antoinette, which I answered, leaving out the most sordid details. It was a rehearsal for the next day when I would have to speak to Madame Théodore and answer some of the same questions. That was a conversation I dreaded.

Charlotte, having eaten her fill, insisted we save the rest of our meal for Antoinette. Angry as I was at Antoinette, I still hadn't the heart to deny Charlotte's wish.

24

Madame Théodore

*E*arly Monday morning I arrived at the Opéra before the other students and sought out Madame Théodore. She greeted me with arms folded over her chest and a deep frown. "*Eh bien*, Marie! Explain yourself, *s'il vous plaît*."

I had carefully rehearsed what I planned to say: *Antoinette is experiencing some difficulties. She regrets that she is unable to attend, and I am trying to help her. We beg for your patience.* But the little speech flew out of my head. I tried to choke back tears, gave in to them, and covered my face with my hands. Madame Théodore led me to her private cubicle near the dressing rooms. She put her arms around me and held me until I stopped weeping. "Troubles?" she asked gently.

I managed to say only, "Antoinette."

She nodded. "*Oui*, I understand," she said. "There has been talk. Come, sit down."

I perched on the edge of a stool and stared miserably at the floor. Madame Théodore was silent for a moment, studying her folded hands. "Now, tell me, Marie. How long will Antoinette be . . . away?"

"Three months."

Madame Théodore shook her head. "Regrettable. She had a promising future with the Opéra ballet, but this means the end of her career. I'm sure she realizes that."

"*Oui*, Madame," I murmured, although I wasn't sure Antoinette did yet fully realize what would happen to her, or if she even cared.

The teacher leaned forward, speaking earnestly. "Truthfully, Marie, I'm more concerned about *you*. You know that we have strict rules about absences, do you not?"

"*Oui*, Madame."

"You already have several on your record. Even worse, the spring examinations are on Friday—in just four days. Will you be prepared? I'm afraid that you won't do well under the circumstances."

"Oh, but I will, Madame! I promise you!" I forced myself to meet her eyes.

"*Bien*," she said. "For the moment I will take you at your word." She smiled and leaned back in her chair. "But not all of the gossip has been unpleasant," she said. "No doubt you've heard that you're the most talked-about dancer in Paris."

I gazed at her blankly.

"I mean, of course, Monsieur Degas's sculpture *Petite danseuse,*" she explained.

The sculpture? Since Antoinette's arrest I had scarcely given a thought to the statuette, which had had such a profound effect on me only a short time ago. "People say she's ugly," I said. "They say terrible things about her."

"It's true that some people are shocked and don't like the statuette or have anything good to say about it. But others, I hear, are fairly swooning in rapture. I myself haven't yet seen it."

"The statuette has nothing to do with me," I said. "It's Monsieur Degas's work. I'm glad if some people like it." I didn't mention that I had seen the statuette, for that would have meant explaining that Lucien Daudet had taken me to the exhibition, and I didn't want to bring up the subject of Lucien.

"You're right," said Madame Théodore. "All of Paris may be talking about you, but you'll likely reap no benefit from your fame." She rose, indicating that our conversation was at an end. "So," she said, "time now for class." She briskly swept me out of the room.

I WORKED HARDER than ever during the morning class, but the moment we were allowed to leave for our midday break, I snatched up the bundle I had put aside and left the Palais Garnier, hoping my absence would be brief. I planned to rush to the prison, leave the bundle with Antoinette, and rush back without being more than a few minutes late for the afternoon rehearsal.

In the bundle was a change of underclothing, a bit of soap, and an old towel, and the remaining half of the eel pie and two slices of melon. But again I had to wait until the iron doors swung open to admit visitors. Once the items had passed the inspection of the matron—a doughy woman with a large wart on her chin from which several black hairs sprouted—I pushed them through the bars of Antoinette's cell. She looked even worse than before.

"I can't stay long, and I don't know when I'll be back," I said. "The examinations are on Friday. I need the extra practice session tomorrow afternoon."

"Oh, Marie!" Antoinette coaxed. "Promise me you'll come tomorrow. You have no idea what it's like here."

"I'll try," I said and hurried away, ignoring her pleas.

A cold spring drizzle had begun to fall, and the cobblestones were slippery. By the time I reached the Palais Garnier, my practice clothes were thoroughly soaked. I was very late—the dancers were all on the stage for the afternoon rehearsal, and I could hear Monsieur Perrot's wooden staff thumping the floor. Wet and shivering, I huddled in the *coulisses*, wondering if I could slip unnoticed into my place. But then I noticed that my place had already been taken by another dancer.

Monsieur Perrot saw me and scolded me in front of everyone. "No dancing tonight," he said.

"*Mais,* Monsieur—," I began. If I didn't dance in tonight's performance, I would have another black mark on my record. And I would be fined for missing the afternoon rehearsal as well.

"No dancing tonight!" the ballet master thundered. I slunk off the stage and back out into the rain.

MADAME THÉODORE said nothing when I appeared Tuesday morning for class, but I knew that she was watching me closely. Grimly I worked through all the exercises at the *barre* and in the center, and after most of the others had left in the afternoon, I stayed on, practicing my jumps. *Only three more days until the examinations:* The thought was constantly on my mind.

Antoinette was also on my mind. On good days Maman managed to put in a few hours at the laundry, but good days were infrequent, and a sensible conversation with her nearly impossible. "Could you visit Antoinette and take her some food?" I had asked the night before, and Maman answered with helpless sighs and mumbled excuses.

Although I carefully hoarded the francs in Antoinette's little leather purse, the money was already running low. The rent would soon fall due. Earlier that spring, before I had learned of the death of Lucien's mother, I had sold the earrings he'd given me, but I still had two pieces: the amethyst necklace and the opal ring. I took the necklace to the dealer and got what I could for it, enough for a reprieve—a month, maybe two, if I managed carefully.

ALTHOUGH I WAS present for my morning class and afternoon rehearsal on Wednesday, I danced poorly at the Wednesday night performance. Even my friends noticed. "We all have our bad days," Mathilde said sympathetically.

"We know you have troubles," murmured Geneviève.

Then Suzanne, the dancer we all envied, fluttered by. "At least you didn't knock anyone down!" she said, laughing.

"Don't say such things," Léonie chided her. Léonie turned to me and said, "Come with us. We'll go to the Rat and have some coffee. My treat."

But I shook my head and went home alone, too disheartened to be with anyone.

THURSDAY MORNING Madame Théodore called me into her cubicle before the beginning of class. "Marie," she said. "I don't have to tell you that you danced very poorly last night. You know, do you not, that you are headed for disaster?"

I nodded miserably. "*Oui*, Madame."

"The examinations are tomorrow. Under ordinary circumstances I should not allow you to take them. I've watched you at rehearsals, and although your talent is evident, you've lost something. You are not concentrating, your mind is else-where, and it shows. Short of a miracle, I don't believe you will pass your examinations. Furthermore, with all the absences on your record, the judges are almost certain to dismiss you."

"*Oui*, Madame, I know, but I *believe* in miracles! There's still a chance, isn't there? You must let me try!" I cried. "Dancing is my life!"

Madame Théodore picked a speck of lint from her black skirt. "All right, Marie," she said. "I will let you try. Perhaps this afternoon I can work with you. We'll have a little extra practice session."

I felt my throat close. "Madame," I managed to croak, "I cannot. I must go to the prison with food for Antoinette."

"And it must be done then? Why not later, after your practice?"

"The matron only allows visitors for one hour in the afternoon. She's very strict."

"*Eh bien*, Marie," she said, her usually stern face creased with concern. "So be it. But you'd better pray for your miracle."

I HAD LITTLE to take to Antoinette on Thursday afternoon, nothing but a roll, a piece of cheese, and a few radishes. "This is the best I can do for now," I said. "But I'll come back Sunday."

Instead of being grateful, Antoinette flew into a temper. "That's all you brought? But you helped yourself to the money in my purse, didn't you, you greedy little wretch!"

"How dare you call *me* greedy!" I gasped, sparks of her anger igniting mine. "You are surely the most miserably selfish creature God ever put on this earth! Because of what you've done, you've lost your position at the Opéra, and now I'm certain to be dismissed as well. If you care nothing about yourself or about me, then think of Charlotte—how do you expect her to continue when she has nothing to eat? Because of you, we'll all be out in the street."

My raving was interrupted by the arrival of the matron, who seized me by both arms and half dragged me to the gates of the prison. "Don't come back here if you can't keep a civil tongue in your head, you guttersnipe," she said, as she sent me sprawling into the muddy prison yard.

For this I had given up Madame Théodore's kind offer to help me prepare for the examinations. "I'm sorry that you're my sister!" I shouted at the fortresslike walls of the prison— but there was no one to hear.

25

Final Examinations

On Friday morning Maman claimed to be too ill to accompany us to the examinations. It was the first time she had ever missed them. Perhaps she was simply too downhearted, too besieged by troubles, to risk witnessing another daughter's failure. But since her behavior had become so unpredictable, I felt relieved that she had chosen to stay at home.

So it was just the two of us, Charlotte and I, who walked together to the Palais Garnier on Friday morning, our footsteps dragging. The walk seemed much longer than usual, and we had little to say, not even bothering with our usual reading lesson. We had kept each other awake for almost the whole night with our restless tossing.

"I was praying," Charlotte confided.

"Ah, your prayers are sure to be answered—you'll do beautifully," I assured her. "You always do."

"I was praying for *you*," she whispered.

I bit my lip to stop the quivering.

We went to the dressing room to change into the new practice tutus given out for the spring examinations. All the dancers' little superstitions came into play at these times. Mathilde stitched new ribbons on her *pointe* shoes. Geneviève pinned an amulet inside her bodice. Léonie worried that her new tutu might actually have been worn once before by a dancer who had not passed her examinations. "What bad luck that would be," she grumbled, "to inherit the tutu of a failed dancer!"

Usually I laughed at my friends' notions, but that morning I did not. When Madame Théodore passed out the numbers to be pinned to our bodices, I accepted number seven reluctantly. I had always disliked that number.

Some dancers silent, some chattering nervously, we rushed down the corridor to our practice room to begin our warm-up exercises.

I had spent the weeks before Antoinette's arrest working hard at the jumps and leg beats I knew would be required of the *coryphées*. We would be judged on our *entrechats* in four, a straight-up jump from fifth position in which the feet change positions, back and forth, four times. The higher one leaped, the more changes one could accomplish. Mine had been very good, flawless, in fact; I could often do six changes. Although I knew that I was not at my best and that a practice session the previous day might have improved my chances, I hoped that somehow I would be good enough. Maybe, I thought, I could do even better than the judges expected, and that would overcome my poor attendance record.

Onstage the *quadrille* dancers finished and waited to hear the judges' verdict. I turned away as they came off, unable to bear the look of pain on the faces of those who had not passed. Then it was our turn.

I was in the fourth group of *coryphées,* with Mathilde and Léonie. We entered on *pointe* with tiny *piqué* steps, performed an *assemblé battu*—a jump with beats—and then positioned ourselves for a series of *entrechats* in four. I decided to do six changes, to impress the judges. That was a mistake. I was out of practice and failed to achieve the necessary elevation; as a result, my landings were not clean. The rest of the required movements went well enough, but I knew that the faulty *entrechats* would count against me.

And so I made a desperate decision: Although it was not scheduled, I decided to add another jump—a *cabriole.* The *cabriole* is a very difficult jump—one leg raised in the air, the other brought up to beat against it at the height of the leap—and one that is often called for in male roles. But the judges had a strict rule: A dancer was not permitted to add anything to the steps required. Occasionally dancers who were determined to advance from *petit sujet* to *premier sujet* broke this rule and succeeded, but it was an enormous risk. I decided to take that risk.

I performed two beautiful *cabrioles* with elegant landings. Grinning with relief—I knew they were good, nearly perfect—I prepared to leave the stage.

"Number seven! Number seven!" called the head judge. "Step forward, *s'il vous plaît!*"

I glanced at Madame Théodore, who was frowning, and walked to the apron of the stage. The three judges sat in the front row of the orchestra.

"Mademoiselle Marie van Goethem?" asked a judge—a fleshy man with droopy mustaches. I nodded. "It is noted that your record shows excessive absences. Poor landings observed on the *entrechats*. Refusal to follow the rules of the examination, which do not allow examinees to alter the program. The jury therefore finds cause to dismiss you from the ballet school of the Paris Opéra." The judge glanced up at me from beneath bushy gray eyebrows. "Regrettable, Mademoiselle, for your *cabrioles* were superb."

Trembling, I performed a deep *révérence* to the judges and the *abonnés* sitting behind them, the last I would ever make, and ran from the stage before the tears started.

THE OTHER DANCERS, unwilling to come close to one so ill-fated, shied away from me as I rushed through the wings, but Madame Théodore caught up to me and grasped my shoulders tightly.

"Oh, Marie, I had such fond dreams for you," she said sadly. "I truly believed that you had a great future as a dancer. And now it's surely over."

She kissed me on both cheeks, and then she let me go.

I handed over the new tutu to the costume mistress, wondering if my bad luck would be passed on to another dancer. I felt as though my heart had been ripped open as I walked out of the Palais Garnier, away from the Opéra *corps de ballet* forever. *Over. Everything I've dreamed of. Finished.*

Charlotte was waiting for me. For her sake I attempted a smile, but she knew it was false and began to sob. We walked slowly home, weeping, our arms around each other.

26

Rue des Martyrs

If it had not been for the promise I made to Papa on his deathbed to try to keep the family together, I would have left Antoinette to rot in Prison Saint-Lazare. But from a sense of duty, I returned three or four times a week. Antoinette never asked about Charlotte or Maman, but she now instructed me to bring extra food for her cell mates. "We've become great friends," she explained.

"I can't," I said. "I can barely feed the three of us. Because of *you*," I reminded her.

She had the grace to look repentant. "I'll make it up to you," she said again. "I promise."

The day after I failed the dance examinations, I began to make the rounds, applying at Théâtre des Variétés and other theaters with dance companies. I was always turned away, often rudely. After a few weeks I had no choice but to take whatever work the laundresses would give me—stoking the charcoal fires under the huge washtubs, pushing wet linens through the wringers, dumping dirty wash water into the gutter. I worked long, wretched hours for one franc a day. I hated my life, I bitterly resented Antoinette, and for the first time I thought I understood why Maman had fallen under the spell of absinthe.

I missed dancing and the excitement of performing on the enormous stage of the Palais Garnier. I missed Madame Théodore's strict discipline, and long hours of practice, and even the visits to the *foyer de la danse*. More than ever, I missed Jean-Pierre, who had been gone now for six months. I had not realized it would be so hard.

In early summer I took Charlotte on the omnibus to the Bois de Boulogne. We returned to the lake where the boat had tipped over, where we had tumbled into the water, but it made me feel worse than ever. Some of my old friends from the Opéra invited me to go with them to the Moulin de la Galette on a Sunday afternoon, but their gossip made me homesick for my former life, and being there reminded me of Jean-Pierre. Everything reminded me of Jean-Pierre!

At the beginning of July, Antoinette was released from prison. She came home and stayed only long enough to pack up her trunk; she was accompanied by a hard-looking man who carried it down for her. She had taken rooms with two of her Saint-Lazare cell mates. "I'll send you money when I can," she said, but I knew better than to count on her promises. When I asked how she intended to earn money now that she was no longer a dancer at the Opéra, she only laughed and looked away. I suspected the worst. I was not sorry to see her go. I had only bitter feelings for Antoinette, and I doubted that she had any feelings at all for us.

A week later the rent collector nailed an eviction notice to our door. Taking the few francs that were left from the sale of the amethyst necklace, I began looking for another place to live. With Antoinette gone, we didn't really need two rooms; Maman and Charlotte and I could make do with one. The room I found on Rue des Martyrs was a hovel with only a single narrow slit of a window, and the stink of rotting garbage rising from the courtyard, but it was a roof over our heads.

A MONTH OR TWO passed, and things only got worse. I had a single piece of jewelry left, the opal ring, which I'd been saving for the day when our circumstances became so dire that I could find no way out. I put the ring in my pocket and made my way across the Seine to the dealer's dim little shop on *la rive gauche*, passing by the entrance to Tante Hélène's workroom. But after a few steps I hesitated, turned back, and climbed the stairs to the door with the silhouette of the dressmaker's dummy. I stood there for a long moment before I turned the handle and entered.

Tante Hélène rushed to greet me, crying, "Marie! Come in, come in!" She led me into the parlor reserved for customers and had me sit down on a little tufted satin divan. She closed the door so that the girls stitching industriously on the other side of the wall couldn't overhear our conversation.

I hadn't seen my aunt since the previous winter. There had been a falling-out between her and Maman when she visited us on Three Kings' Day. The argument had again centered on the future of Maman's daughters. Tante Hélène had left angrily, saying, "I will not come to a place where I'm insulted," and had added that if any of us wished to see her, it was up to us to find her.

I'd thought of going to her for help when Antoinette was sent to prison, but it seemed too humiliating. I'd thought of it again when I was dismissed from the Opéra, but again my pride interfered. What took me there that day was a conversation I had overheard: Charlotte telling Maman she wanted to leave the Opéra and get a job that would pay her more money. That had sickened me, but Maman's reply was even worse: "But if you stay at the Opéra, you're sure to meet some nice gentlemen, like your sisters did." If Charlotte chose either course, I would know that I had failed utterly.

"Now tell me, *ma chère*, what's wrong?" asked Tante Hélène. "You look so very, very sad."

I told her all that had happened, ending with our eviction and move to Rue des Martyrs and my fears for Charlotte. "I haven't enough money to take care of her. I promised Papa I'd take care of her, but I can't!"

Tante Hélène listened carefully to my somber story, and at the end she once again invited me to come to work for her. "I'll train you to become the finest seamstress in all of Paris!" she promised. "If you work hard, you may one day have a couturier business like mine." She offered to pay me as much as I'd been earning at the Opéra. "You could do worse," she reminded me.

By the time I crossed the Seine for the second time that day, I had agreed to Tante Hélène's offer. I would start work the next day. She had pressed two francs into my palm to help us until I was paid. I would not have to sell Lucien's opal ring just yet.

THE AIR IN Tante Hélène's workroom was stifling. We worked thirteen hours a day, six days a week: from seven in the morning until eight at night. Although I tried diligently to master the skills of dressmaking, I had no talent. I was clumsy with the shears, bled on the fabric when I pricked my fingers, and let dainty pearl buttons drop into the cracks between the floorboards. By the end of the day, my eyes burned, my neck ached, and my head throbbed.

The girls in the workroom seemed a dull lot. They wouldn't have lasted a day—an hour!—at the Opéra ballet, under the stern eye and sharp tongue of Madame Théodore. Their silly chatter annoyed me, maybe because they made no attempt to include me. To keep my mind occupied, I tried to recall every detail of the dances I had performed, hearing in my head the music of Meyerbeer, Delibes, and Bizet, and mentally executing the intricate steps. I escaped into daydreams of the roles I still hoped, by some miracle, to dance one day—imagining my dramatic entrances, my thrilling *tours jetés* and *cabrioles*, the subtle gestures I'd make to convey each character's intense feelings.

Many times, though, my fantasies were not about dancing. They were about Jean-Pierre. I made a game of trying to remember every time we'd been together and of imagining what it would be like when we were together again. He'd promised to come back. But when? I touched the medal of Saint Christophe that he'd given me, and ached with longing.

When I was most deeply caught up in my reveries, my hand hung motionless above the dress I was supposed to be sewing, until Tante Hélène's harsh voice broke the spell: "Marie! Pay attention, *s'il vous plaît*!"

Walking home in the evenings to our dreary room, I avoided passing near the Opéra. My footsteps were leaden— I, who could once leap higher than any of the other *coryphées*, could scarcely lift my feet. It seemed that everywhere I went, I encountered some deeply painful memory.

CHARLOTTE, now eleven, begged me to come to the autumn dance examinations. I had to tell her I could not. "Tante Hélène won't give me time off," I said, although I hadn't bothered to ask. The truth was, I didn't have the heart to enter the Palais Garnier. But on the day of the examinations Maman again claimed to be too weak to leave her bed. I decided to accompany Charlotte after all, recognizing that my tender feelings for her were stronger than the pain of my own loss.

The sky was clear and a fresh breeze lifted the little blond curls framing Charlotte's pale face. I felt her tense excitement as we entered the Palais Garnier—my first time inside that building in six months. I kissed Charlotte and wished her luck and went to look for a seat in the *grande salle de spectacle* behind the orchestra pit, as far as possible from the judges. Madame Théodore and the violinist had already taken their places on the stage when Monsieur Degas entered, nodding to a few of the *abonnés* who'd been invited to attend. Among them was Lucien Daudet. I slumped in my seat and lowered my head in case he looked my way.

As soon as Charlotte and her group finished executing their steps—Charlotte performed beautifully—I slipped out of the *grande salle* and hurried backstage to wait for her. She emerged flushed and thrilled, having learned that she'd passed with distinction. I was happy for her, of course, but miserable for myself.

Still, Charlotte deserved to celebrate. I had in my pocket a couple of francs saved from the previous week's wages, and I proposed that we go to the Nouvelle-Athènes for lunch. "I wish Antoinette had been there," Charlotte said, enjoying her dish of stew. We had not spoken of our sister for some time. "I wonder what she's doing."

"I don't know," I said, although I thought I did.

After our lunch I hurried back to the workroom. Tante Hélène was angry at first, until I explained the circumstances. She would deduct from my wages, of course, but she didn't threaten me with a fine or with the loss of my position, and we went on as before.

27

Little Dancer Aged Fourteen

The golden days of autumn faded into the muted browns and grays of early winter. The sun disappeared and the cold rains began. Then one day, as I was bent over my needlework, squinting at the tiny stitches—I had finally learned to make them fine and even—Tante Hélène answered a knock at the door. I looked up, curious about what new customer might be arriving. Jean-Pierre, blushing deeply, stepped into the workroom. I dropped the skirt I'd been hemming, too surprised to speak.

"Marie," he said. "I've been looking everywhere for you."

Reaching for my shawl, I followed Jean-Pierre out of the salon without a word.

Our embrace at the top of the stairs—tearful on my part, exuberant on his—is one I'll always remember. Once we could bear to break apart, we ran through sheets of chilling rain to a café on the Quai de Conti. As people on the other side of the steamy windows hurried by with umbrellas, Jean-Pierre told me his story.

He had reached his family's farm near Rouen a few days after Christmas to learn that his father had died only hours earlier. For the first weeks after the funeral he helped his mother get their affairs in order. The farm had fallen into neglect, and he'd spent the winter fixing farm equipment and repairing the house and the cow barn. In the spring he and his younger brothers mended fences to keep the sheep from wandering off, plowed the fields, and planted. In late summer he harvested the crops, and in early autumn he made wine from the abundant grape yield, and butchered a cow. In his spare time he worked on an old stone house at the edge of the property, turning it from a ruined shell without a roof or windows into a pretty little house looking out over the green hills, toward Rouen in the distance.

"And always I thought of you, Marie. The drawing that you gave me when I left? It hangs above my bed. I talked to it every night, telling it my hopes and dreams! Then last week I left for Paris."

On the night he arrived, he'd gone to the Palais Garnier, looking for me. He waited and waited, he said, but neither I nor Antoinette came out.

"What about Charlotte? Surely you must have seen her?"

But somehow, he had not.

He'd gone then to our old rooms on Rue de Douai, where he'd found new tenants. He'd stopped at the tobacconist's shop and asked Monsieur Lerat what had become of us. All the tobacconist could tell him was that we had simply disappeared. I regretted that I had not even said good-bye to Monsieur Lerat. He'd always been especially kind to me— but I didn't want him to pass the information along to the rent collector or anyone else who might come to dun us for unpaid debts. Jean-Pierre had even gone by the laundry, but Maman worked only irregularly and no one there was willing to tell him anything.

"And then, Marie, I did the boldest thing of all: I went to Monsieur Degas's studio."

"Surely you didn't!" I exclaimed.

"Surely I did!" he said, laughing. "Climbed up those five flights of stairs and pounded on the door of his studio until he finally opened it. He stared at me through his blue-tinted spectacles and asked my business. I said that I was seeking Mademoiselle Marie van Goethem, who had modeled for him. And he said"—here Jean-Pierre perfectly imitated Monsieur Degas's gravelly voice—"'What I know of her is right here.' And he pointed to a glass case with a statuette. *'Petite danseuse de quatorze ans,'* he said. Even from across the room I could see that it was you, *chérie.*"

Jean-Pierre took my hands in his and kissed my fingertips. "Monsieur Degas gazed at the *Little Dancer* with such tenderness, Marie. 'She is like my daughter,' he said. 'Flesh of my flesh, bone of my bone. I can never part with her.' I understood that he meant it's the sculpture he loves, not the model. Of the model he knows nothing at all."

The rain slackened and finally gave way to watery sunshine, and we left the café. Crossing the Seine, we stopped to gaze down at the river flowing beneath us on its way to the ocean. I thought of the many times I had stood on this bridge, wondering if somewhere far away Jean-Pierre might be standing by the banks of this same river. How lonely I had been then, and how happy I felt now!

"Then how *did* you find me?"

"I was outside the Opéra again just now, looking for you, trying to get up the courage to go inside and inquire, and Charlotte saw me. She told me what had happened and where to find you. I'm so sorry you were dismissed, Marie, but it's so good to be here with you!"

Standing by the river, we embraced again. All the misery of the past months vanished like a puff of smoke as I stood folded in his arms. Now everything would be all right. Now I would be able to endure the long hours in Tante Hélène's workroom, until I could find a position somewhere as a dancer. I sighed contentedly. "Have you gone to see the Cassatts?" I asked.

"*Non*—why should I go to see the Cassatts? It's only you I want to see."

"To get back your old job as their coachman. Or have you other prospects?"

"Prospects? But I have no intention of staying in Paris. That's why I came for you—to ask you to come home with me to Rouen and to be married there."

I felt as though my breath was being squeezed out of me. *Go to Rouen?*

Jean-Pierre was watching me, his blue eyes troubled. "But you do love me, don't you? You promised to wait for me. Is there someone else?"

"*Mais non,* there's no one else. And I do love you, and I have waited for you. But to leave Paris ..." The tiny bubbles of happiness that had been sparkling through me like champagne suddenly vanished, replaced by a tight little knot of doubt.

We had begun walking again. Jean-Pierre's arm was around my waist, pulling me close. "It's beautiful there," he said. "I know that you'll come to love it. The farm is a good one, a home where we can start a good life together, have our children, raise a family. I thought that's what you'd want, Marie. It's what I've been working so hard for all these months." He hesitated, then added, smiling, "My father left me a little money. We could go to America for our honeymoon."

I remembered his dream of going there one day: to New York and San Francisco, and to New Orleans, where they spoke French. How lovely it would be! I struggled against temptation, strived to find the right words.

"I didn't know that you wanted to live in Rouen. I

thought you were coming back to live here, in Paris, that someday we'd marry and have our family here, so that I could dance—"

"But you're *not* dancing! You're no longer at the Opéra! I found you working as a seamstress—surely that's not what you want!" A sharp edge had crept into his voice.

Since I'd been dismissed, I'd clung stubbornly to the notion that I would find my way back to dancing—if not at the Opéra then surely somewhere else. All those years of rigorous training and hard work—for what? To milk cows?

But there was more at stake than my career: Charlotte. She was only eleven—too young to be on her own— Maman was in no condition to look after her, and Antoinette had gone down her own dark path. It was Charlotte who held the most promise. I might never be an *étoile*, but I believed that Charlotte would.

"Charlotte . . . ," I began.

Jean-Pierre interrupted, "She will come with us, of course."

"But she can't! She has real talent! More than I have, more than Antoinette. Of the three of us, she's most likely to make a life of dance. I can't ask her to give that up." The words tumbled out: "I can't marry you, Jean-Pierre, because I can't leave Paris. Maybe in a few years, when Charlotte is on her own, but not now."

"Is that your answer, then, Marie?" The pain was written across his face and showed most clearly in his eyes—eyes that I loved still. But my love for him didn't change my answer.

"Oui, mon amour," I said. "Yes, my love. That is my answer."

I knew that Jean-Pierre could not wait for me. His life was now in Rouen. This time when he left, it would be good-bye: not just *au revoir*—until we meet again—but *adieu,* a final farewell.

Standing on the Pont Neuf, we embraced and kissed for the last time. Jean-Pierre turned away and strode off, head down, toward the other side of the river. I couldn't bear to watch him go. The rain had begun again. I turned and walked in the opposite direction, back to Tante Hélène's workroom, my heart breaking, my eyes blinded by tears. I felt as though I had finally lost everything. I had nothing more to lose.

Paris, 1882

28

The Cimetière de Montmartre

Through the deep cold of the winter months that followed Jean-Pierre's visit, I wondered many times if I had made the right decision. While I toiled hour after hour at needlework that I despised, then went home to shiver in our wretched hovel, I often pictured him, snug by the fire in the stone hearth of the home he had made for us. Sometimes I could even picture myself beside him, an image I had to banish quickly, before I began to weep.

Then spring came, as it always does, and Charlotte, now twelve, was promoted to the *quadrille*. In the summer Antoinette paid us a surprise visit, nostrils flaring as she glanced around at our squalid surroundings. She arrived decked out in expensive-looking blue silk, fashionable boots, and a fetching little bonnet. It was apparent that she was expecting a child.

Although I was seething—that she had abandoned us, had never made good on her promise to send us any money—I managed to say nothing, waiting instead for her to tell us whatever it was she had to say.

"I'm living quite nicely now, as you can see. I have a new lover, a gentleman with an important position in the government, and he provides well for me. Three pretty little rooms on Rue Véron, and a cook! He brings friends to dine quite often, and on those occasions I also have a footman. It's not as grand as I'd like, but not bad. But, as you can see, I've got a little problem here." She glanced at her bulging belly and grimaced. "A *great* inconvenience, believe me."

"*Oui*, I can see that," I said through clenched teeth. "When is it due?"

"September." She sighed. "I'm wondering if you and Maman could take care of it after it's born. I'd pay you, of course." She smiled winningly.

"Are you mad?" I cried, no longer able to remain calm. "How dare you suggest that I become your child's nursemaid! Have you forgotten that my visits to you at Prison Saint-Lazare caused my dismissal from the Opéra?" I was shouting now. "Maman is unfit to care for an infant—she wasn't fit to care for us! And you expect *me* to do it? I'm working for Tante Hélène, as I thought you knew."

"I suppose I'd forgotten," she replied blandly, apparently unperturbed by my outburst. "Does she pay you well?"

"Well enough," I said, more calmly.

"*Eh bien,* whatever it is, I'll pay you more."

"*Non, non, non,*" I said. "Absolutely not! Besides, this is no place for a child. It's scarcely fit to live in. I can't even offer you a decent place to sit."

She didn't disagree. "If you change your mind, come let me know. But don't wait too long. By the way, I've left a little something on the table for you. A token." She swept out the door and down the filthy stairs, her skirts lifted high.

"You would do well to make other plans," I called after her. On the table I saw five francs spread out. I grabbed them and threw the coins down the stairs after her, slamming the door, determined to put my sister out of my mind. Charlotte found four of the five francs when she came home. The fifth one had rolled away.

TWO MONTHS LATER Antoinette sent a messenger to Tante Hélène's workroom, with a note she had dictated to a friend: She had given birth to a daughter. The baby was robust and healthy, but my sister had developed a fever. "Come, come as soon as you can, I beg you. My life hangs by a thread, and I don't want to die without your forgiveness."

I read the note to Tante Hélène. "What should I do? Antoinette has a way of altering the truth to get what she wants."

My aunt replied, "You must go for the sake of the baby."
When I hesitated, she added, "I'll go with you." We closed
the shop early and hurried to Rue Véron, in Montmartre.

Antoinette's green eyes blazed feverishly, and her cheeks
were flushed and hot to my touch. The baby slept in a little
cot by her bedside.

"Marie," she whispered, "I'm afraid I'm going to die."

"Nonsense, you're just weak from the delivery," I said.
But my aunt breathed close to my ear, "I fear she's right."

"What do you think of her? The baby?" Antoinette asked
feebly. "She's beautiful, isn't she?"

"*Oui,* like her mother."

"Did I tell you her name? It's Louise. For Maman."

"Maman will be pleased."

"Will you ask her to come? Tell her I want to see her.
Charlotte, too."

"I will," I promised.

A wet nurse took the sleeping infant away, and Tante
Hélène began to bustle around, preparing poultices to place
over my sister's womb to reduce the swelling, and brewing
teas that she thought would bring down the fever.

"It happens to many women after childbirth. No one
knows what causes it, and there's no cure. We can only wait
and pray."

I sat by Antoinette's bedside, stroking her hand. "The father?" I asked gently. "Does he know?"

She shook her head and drifted into restless sleep. While

she slept, I hurried home to tell Maman and Charlotte what had happened. Maman made a great effort to struggle out of bed, and Charlotte and I helped her climb the steep hill to Rue Véron. My mother and my aunt nodded to each other, coolly at first—and then clung to each other, weeping. I placed the swaddled infant Louise in Charlotte's arms, and Charlotte promptly fell in love with her newborn niece.

That night I stayed with Antoinette after the others had gone, having promised to send for them if her condition worsened. Hour after hour through the long night I sat by her bedside, stroking her brow and changing the napkins that quickly became blood soaked. Once, she emerged from her fever and gripped my hand. "Marie," she said. "I've been very selfish, and I know I've treated you badly. I'm sorry. Forgive me—*je t'en prie*—I beg you."

"I forgive you," I whispered, and she closed her eyes.

Sometime before dawn I must have dozed. When the baby's cries woke me at first light, I touched my sister's pale face. It was cold as marble.

Antoinette was dead.

I WAS NOW responsible for a tiny life. I took the last of Lucien Daudet's gifts, the opal ring, and made a final visit to the dealer.

"This is the last time I will come here," I said, glaring at him menacingly. "I believe you've cheated me in the past, but you will not dare to cheat me now. An infant's life depends on this."

The dealer glanced at me warily and used his jeweler's loupe to study the quality of the gem. He counted out a hundred francs and spread them on the counter. I waited, arms folded, silent. He added ten more francs to the pile. *"Merci,"* I said, scooping up the money.

It was enough to move us into better rooms on *la rive gauche,* close to Tante Hélène's workroom. Maman, enchanted with her tiny granddaughter, found the strength to pull herself together enough to find a position, for a few hours a week, with a nearby laundry. The four of us— Maman, Tante Hélène, Charlotte, and I—managed to take care of a baby who brought us all joy.

LIFE MOVED ON for all of us. I became much more skillful with the needle and began to take over some of my aunt's business. Maman's health once again worsened, and death came for her just before Louise's third birthday. Soon after that, I paid a visit to our old neighborhood and stopped at the tobacconist's shop to say hello to Monsieur Lerat. Nearly his old self again, he came out from behind the counter and engulfed me in a great bear hug.

"Ah, Marie, Marie, I'm glad to see you! Come, tell me everything that's happened. Everything!"

I laughed, and told him a little.

"Come back soon," he said as I was leaving. "I've missed you."

And so I did go back, and gradually I got into the habit of stopping by to see him, with Louise. Whenever I did, he would close the shop, link his arm in mine, and take us to the Café de la Nouvelle-Athènes for coffee—and a sweet for my niece. One thing led to another, and eventually, after a year or so, he proposed marriage.

I thought it over carefully. I still sometimes dreamed of Jean-Pierre, but Alphonse Lerat was kind, gentle, and generous. Although he was much older than I, his two boys nearly grown, I allowed myself to be persuaded. We were married in the Lady Chapel of Notre-Dame de Lorette. Years passed, and although we had no children of our own, Louise was enough for us. I thought of her as my daughter, and I was not unhappy.

Perhaps my greatest triumph, though, was Charlotte, who came to live with my new family. I always made it a point to attend the twice-yearly examinations as she was promoted regularly through the ranks of the *corps de ballet,* achieving the position of *coryphée* and then *sujet.* Monsieur Degas discovered her and asked her to pose for him. By the time she was eighteen, she was being chosen for small solo parts.

Perhaps my proudest moment came the night I saw her dance the role of Eros in the ballet *Sylvia.* Not only did she dance the part to perfection, but she inhabited the character of Eros in a way that I could not have imagined. From her first entrance I was so moved that Alphonse, who had been setting aside an extra franc now and then to pay for our tickets, worried that I wouldn't be able to see her properly through my tears.

"The sacrifice was worth it, worth everything," I murmured, leaning on his arm as we made our way home that night.

"Ah, *oui, bien sûr,*" he said kindly, patting my hand. "We'll come to see her again."

He had mistaken my meaning. The sacrifice I meant was not the occasional price of a ticket but the forfeit of my own dreams. My reward was the chance to see my sister become *une étoile*—not one of the most brilliant stars in the universe, but a star, nevertheless. Charlotte was a mainstay of the Paris Opéra ballet for years, and after she retired from dancing she became a teacher at the ballet school. I often spoke to her of our much-feared and equally loved Madame Théodore.

"Madame Théodore once told me my *attitude* looked like *un chien pissant,*" I said one time. "I didn't forgive her for years."

Charlotte laughed. "We all tell our students that," she said. "Because it's true!"

Our niece, Louise, had no interest in becoming a dancer. Charlotte and I were both disappointed, but one cannot live someone else's life. Louise went to work in the patisserie below Mademoiselle Cassatt's old studio and married one of the pastry makers when she was just nineteen. The following year, 1903, I welcomed a grandniece, Lucie.

Sometimes, as we strolled past Place Pigalle or along the streets of Montmartre, Alphonse and I caught sight of Monsieur Degas, old and frail, his cane tucked under his arm, walking "like a duck," as Jean-Pierre used to say.

I'VE COME AT LAST to the end of my story.

Yesterday, the twenty-seventh of September, 1917, Edgar Degas died, an old man of eighty-three.

The funeral was held this morning, a warm and lovely Saturday filled with brilliant autumn sunshine. We gathered in the church of Saint Jean l'Évangeliste in Montmartre—— a little crowd of perhaps a hundred friends and admirers, and maybe even a few former models, who remember him fondly. I recognized among them a distinguished white-haired woman dressed in elegant black: Mademoiselle Mary Cassatt, who remained his friend for many years. Following a simple service, the funeral procession made its slow, somber way to the Cimetière de Montmartre, and the coffin was interred in the Degas family crypt.

I sometimes think of the hours I spent posing for the statuette *Petite danseuse de quatorze ans*. In the beginning she created quite a scandal. People said terrible things about her, and about me! Only one critic, writing in an obscure art journal, offered unqualified praise: "In the long history of sculpture there is nothing quite like *Petite danseuse*," he wrote. "She is so real that one would not be surprised to see her open the door of her glass cage and stalk away from prying eyes." The article was signed simply "L. D." Lucien Daudet? Perhaps.

But her fame spread, and the *Little Dancer* became recognized as a masterpiece, prized by collectors. I understand that Monsieur Degas received many offers for his statuette, but he refused to sell it. I hear that she's still somewhere in his studio, in fourth position, head tilted, eyes half closed, hands clasped behind her back.

How strange life is, *non?* Strange and beautiful, like Monsieur Degas's art.

Author's Note

Petite danseuse de quatorze ans—*Little Dancer Aged Fourteen*—is the only sculpture Edgar Degas ever exhibited during his lifetime, although in the years that followed the 1881 Sixth Exhibition of Independent Artists, he created many more small sculptures of his favorite subjects: dancers, horses, and women bathing. He considered the sculptures studies for his pictures, not works of art in themselves, and showed them only to his friends and to other artists.

Degas was among a group of late nineteenth-century painters living in Paris who rebelled against the rigidity of the standards by which French art was judged. The painters were labeled *impressionists* by a disgruntled art critic who ridiculed their use of light and color as well as the content of their work. Degas's artist-friends included Édouard Manet,

Paul Cézanne, Auguste Renoir, Claude Monet, Camille Pissarro, Gustave Caillebotte, and of course, the American artist Mary Cassatt—whose status as a woman prohibited her from frequenting the cafés where the others met to drink coffee, smoke, and plan their exhibitions.

Degas's reputation was well established, even before the exhibitions. His portraits, pictures of café life, and luminous portrayals of ballet dancers, which broke the old rules of perspective and balance, were much in demand by collectors. But his sculpture *Petite danseuse* shocked even his admirers and brought him both ridicule and praise.

When Degas's heirs visited his studio after his death, they found dozens of small sculptures in wax and clay, most of them broken and badly deteriorated. The heirs chose seventy-three of the best-preserved pieces and took them to a maker of bronze castings, who produced twenty-two sets of bronzes, using the complex lost wax process. Today about thirteen hundred individual bronzes can be accounted for, including, of course, several copies of the *Little Dancer*, always in a real tutu. These bronzes are part of major museums' collections throughout the world.

Although photographs of Degas's most famous masterpiece appear in art books, they cannot compare with the sculpture itself. I first saw *Petite danseuse* at an exhibition in Rochester, New York, in December 2002, and was immediately entranced by it. I still am.

Numerous books have been written about Edgar Degas, but little is known of Marie van Goethem and her family. No historical evidence of her life, or of Antoinette's, exists following Antoinette's arrest and imprisonment and Marie's dismissal from the Paris Opéra. Only Charlotte continued her career in ballet, moving up through the ranks to become a *sujet*. In 1907 Charlotte van Goethem ended her career as a dancer and became a professor at the ballet school at the Opéra; she retired in 1933.

But the girl who was the model for the *Little Dancer* continues to fascinate museumgoers, art historians, and contemporary dancers. In April 2003 a new ballet opened at the Palais Garnier titled *La petite danseuse de Degas*—created by Martine Kahane, archivist and curator, and Patrice Bart, choreographer, both of the Paris Opéra. At last, 122 years later, Marie became *une étoile*, a star.

When Degas's sculpture *Little Dancer Aged Fourteen* was first revealed, the audience was not expecting the piece to so realistically show the stress, strain, and tension of a ballerina's life. The original work, now exhibited in the Louvre in Paris, was created in wax in about 1880–81. It was made even more lifelike by Degas's special additional touches: ballet shoes, a real bodice covered in wax, a tutu of muslin, and a wig made of hair and tied with a silk ribbon. This version, cast in bronze in the 1920s from the original wax sculpture, is painted and adorned with muslin and silk.